BULL AND ME

BY

MARY KERR

COPYRIGHT 2016

Chapter One

Janet led me out the back door of her office, down a long, dark corridor and out into the private parking garage. She carried one of my bags. I had the other two. She popped the trunk with her fob and we loaded my suitcases. I pulled the bill of my baseball cap down and turned up my collar to hide my profile. My actions are those of a criminal but I'm innocent. I'm escaping a criminal—I hope. That's the plan. Get me safely out of town and hide me someplace so Roy can't beat me to a pulp or kill me.

"Get in the back and stay down," she ordered, as she climbed into the driver's seat.

I felt the car lurch to the driver's side under her weight. Janet is two hundred pounds plus of no-nonsense, tough lady. She is my attorney in one of the more notorious divorces in the recent history of Harris County. Several prior divorces of the prominent in Houston have culminated in murder. That's what we are trying to circumvent today, my demise. The most hideous details of our hostile divorce were publicized on the cover of the Stargazer, the local rag mag.

The magazine's photographer had ambushed me as I stepped out of a cab at the emergency room the evening Roy assaulted me. My swollen, bleeding face made the cover, in color. That was the worst Roy had ever beaten me. Before that, it was a shove he claimed afterward was playful. The shoves became slaps, accidentally too hard, he'd say to apologize as he gave me yet another bauble to make my anger and fear go away, lulling me back into the marriage.

From the emergency room, I checked into a hotel and

called Janet as soon as her office opened the next morning. When Roy discovered my whereabouts, I was inundated with flowers. I returned from Janet's office to find a dozen bouquets of my favorite gardenias filling my suite with their cloying scent. I notified the desk downstairs not to accept any deliveries on my behalf, floral or otherwise. He could well go from flowers to fists —again.

Janet's first act was a restraining order. She filed the papers for my divorce the same day as her second act. The flowers stopped. The flood of paperwork began. Almost daily, I was served papers of some kind at work. Roy had declared war on me.

For months I had secretly stashed cash. I began hoarding money after he shoved me the first time. A flash of hatred had crossed his handsome face as he pushed me. The look was gone in an instant and I wondered afterward if I'd actually seen it or had it been my imagination? My self-preservation instinct had sparked to life that day nearly a year ago. I had over thirty thousand dollars plus all of the jewelry he'd gifted me with stashed in a flower can at the shop where I worked.

My continuing to work was a problem. Roy fought me but I refused to quit. He'd introduce me.

"This is my wife, Isabelle. She digs dirt."

We had a cook and a maid. There was nothing for me to do in the huge downtown apartment we called home.

"Think of my work as a hobby," I told him. My salary went into the can.

My fear made me huddle on the floor of the car. I wouldn't take a chance on one of Roy's goons spotting me crouched in her back seat if one was on guard at the exit. I should have gotten into the trunk with my luggage. Too late, we're rolling.

Janet hit play on the CD player and Rod Stewart crooned to us as we followed the circular route to the ground floor of the parking garage. She turned up the volume and rolled down her window to speak to the gate keeper.

"Have a good weekend, Domingo. See you Monday."

I heard him answer and heard the barrier lift. We rolled through and took a hard right shooting onto the street and immediately accelerating past the speed limit.

Janet telephoned Domingo before we left her office on the third floor. Domingo would delay the next few cars to exit. The car phone rang.

"Yes, Domingo?" The CD player stopped automatically when the phone rang.

"I see. Thanks."

The car swerved to the left and then turned left.

"We have a tail. He was waiting on the street. I'm afraid you'll have to stay down for awhile. I'm headed for the garage of a friend of mine. We'll swap cars."

The music blared again. Janet sang along with Rod.

I crouched on the floor behind Janet and wondered how I'd ever come to this. How did my life go so wrong?

I came to Houston seeking my fortune. I was fresh out of college at the age of twenty-seven, nearly twenty-eight. Yes, I was older than most graduates. I'd worked my way through school waiting tables and four years had taken me nine. Twice I'd had to sit out an entire year when money was scarce and I worked two jobs to eat, keep a roof over my head and save for school.

I grew up in the foster system. There was no family support, morale-wise or monetary, to lend a hand. I had no roots and could not get student loans. But, I did it. I had my degree in horticulture. I was proud of myself. A large florist shop in the business district was happy to hire me.

That's how I met Macleroy (Roy) McKnight. Roy headed, actually owned, a start-up software company in an office building close to my job. He ordered roses for his secretary and I delivered them. She was gone from her desk. I stood uncertainly, not wanting to leave the expensive blooms on the wrong desk. There was a nameplate, Ms. Parish, but the flowers were ordered for Stephanie, no last name. Thus, my predicament.

"May I help you?"

I wheeled around to face the man who'd stepped out of the office behind the desk. He was very tall, tanned and blond. He smiled and the day brightened as if the sun had come from under a cloud.

"I hope so. I have flowers for Stephanie at this office. Are Ms. Parish and Stephanie one and the same?"

"They are. Those are gorgeous. Did you arrange them?"

He came close and bent to breathe in the fragrance. When he lowered his head, I had a bird's eye view. His hair curled slightly around his ears and on the back of his neck. I could picture him on the beach with long curly locks and a surfboard.

"Nice choice, too. I didn't know what to order." He smiled in gratitude exposing perfect white teeth.

"They are an unusual color combination," I said, standing beside him admiring the pink roses whose petals faded to snow white tips.

"Their scent is spicier." I put my nose to the bouquet and inhaled.

He lowered his head at the same moment and we bumped

heads over the roses. I jerked back, gazed into electric blue eyes and turned red, inside and out. The inside red suffused me with heat.

"I'm so sorry." I felt my forehead expecting a knot to be rising.

"No, my fault. They are spicy." He stared into my eyes.

"Would you like a cup of coffee?" He waved one hand indicating the open door behind him.

"Thank you, I'm all right. I need to hurry back. It's Friday, rush day." I smiled, pivoted on one heel of my ankle-high work boot and rushed away toward the elevator.

When the doors glided shut, I looked down at my dirt-stained knees below the faded Bermuda shorts I'd worn that day. My blouse was frayed khaki that I'd made sleeveless by ripping out the sleeves. I'd intended to spend my day potting plants in the back of Alice's Flower Shoppe, not delivering to hoity-toity addresses in the business district. I was dressed accordingly.

Shirley, the part-time delivery girl, had not showed for work after school and I'd been drafted when the deliveries got too far ahead of Amos. Why couldn't I have been wearing a pretty skirt and blouse, my-out-front-at-the-counter work wear? Just my luck, I met Prince Charming and I looked like Cinderella scouring a sooty hearth. I was smiling at myself when the elevator bumped to a stop on the first floor.

I wasn't just surprised when he showed up at the shop the next week, I was stunned and speechless.

"There's a customer out front who demands your personal services," said Alice, sticking her head through the door from the shop.

I was re-potting some tropical specimens that required TLC.

"Really?"

"Really. He says he only trusts your judgment." She

disappeared inside.

I brushed my hands together knocking off the loose soil. It was probably Harry Fox, an elderly gentleman, who came frequently for flowers for his ailing wife in the nursing home. I pushed a stray lock of curls out of my eyes and went into the shop with a big smile on my face to greet Harry.

The smile froze, as did I, when I saw the man from the office I'd been to last week, not Harry.

"Hello again. I need your expertise, I was explaining to Alice." He smiled his perfect smile.

"I expect it would be easier to ask for you if I knew your name."

"Isabelle. I'm Isabelle," I said, practically stammering. Thank goodness Alice was busy with another customer.

"What do you need?"

"My mother is having a dinner party. I'd like to send her an arrangement for a centerpiece. Is that possible?" He gazed into my eyes, an invisible current in his gaze made my soul shudder.

"Sure. We need a few details. You'll want it to be just right," I told him, as I stepped over behind the counter to fill in an order slip.

"How many people? I'm wondering how large the table will be," I explained.

"Twelve."

"Would you happen to know what color she will use on the table? The linen or place mats, napkins?" I squinted up at him not expecting him to have any idea.

"Mother always uses white table linen, napkins *and* tablecloth."

"That makes my job easier. I don't think many men could have answered that question," I said, with a laugh, "want to try for two?"

"Sure." He smiled.

He likes my game.

Wow!

"Okay. What about china? Have any idea what she'll use?" I raised my brows at him and knocked the curl I'd pushed away earlier back onto my forehead.

"Her china is white, silver edge, and tiny pink roses around the lip. Do I win something? A date with you perhaps?"

Now *my* insides were not the only things heated, his eyes smoldered as he stared in his relentless gaze that saw too much of me.

I took in the expensive suit, the designer silk tie that I'd bet my salary for a week was a one-of-a-kind.

"I'm like Cinderella, in rags, and I don't have a fairy Godmother. I wouldn't be able to dress suitably for a date with you." I leveled with him telling myself it was best to nip this in the bud.

"Let me send you a dancing dress, what size?" He took me in from head to toe with his hot eyes.

My face flushed red showing my embarrassment as well as my temper.

"I beg your pardon. Absolutely not!" I almost shouted.

His gaze flared into something I didn't recognize. If only I'd known the look for what it was back then but hindsight is always too late.

Alice turned to see why I was raising my voice to a customer.

"I'm sorry. Please forgive me. That was a stupid thing to say. I didn't mean to offend you. I'll take you the way you are, beautiful," he said, and he smirked down at me.

"You need to wash your face though."

"Do you still want the flowers?" I'd probably cost Alice a good account.

"Yes, please. Could I take you to lunch? There's a Cafe next door. Show me you forgive me and let me buy you a burger or a bowl of chili. I've eaten there. They make excellent chili." That fabulous smile was back on his face.

"Thank you. You are forgiven. I really don't have time to go out for lunch. I'm in the middle of something delicate. Do you want the centerpiece delivered?"

"Yes."

"Address?"

"Mrs. Virginia McKnight, The Washington Towers, Number 501." He held out a credit card.

"I won't know the exact amount until I finish the arrangement." The name on the card was Macleroy McKnight.

"If you're giving me carte blanche," I added.

"Okay, yes, please go all out," he slipped the card back into the open wallet in his other hand, "bill the office. Don't stint on the arrangement, Mother is particular and she likes to pamper her guests with the best."

"I promise she'll like it," I said. Already in my head I was picturing an arrangement of large waxy white magnolia, small white stephanotis, sprays of baby pink roses so pale they were nearly white in a long narrow mirror-covered container we'd just got in that morning.

"I'm sure she will. Let's have chili next week, pretty please."

"Sure," I agreed to please him.

I planned to soak him good for the arrangement, I wouldn't go so far as to cheat him, but I'd use our most expensive materials and blossoms. At least, that's why I told myself, I agreed. It couldn't be because he makes my heart thump so loud I can hear it.

Chapter Two

Roy called the shop five minutes after we opened Monday morning.

"Mother is your biggest fan. She may be more entranced with you than I am. She wanted to send you flowers until I pointed out how ridiculous that would be," he laughed, a delighted sound, in my ear.

"I hope that means the centerpiece passed muster."

"The centerpiece surpassed the menu. The ladies all requested your name and phone number. Mother put them off, saying she'd have to check. She doesn't want to share you," he said. "I saw the arrangement, Isabelle, it was the most perfect thing I've ever seen—beyond you, of course."

"You're being too kind."

The arrangement had been perfect. Alice took photos before Amos carried it away. She preached at him to be careful before she allowed him to touch it.

The centerpiece was long, three feet long. The height was a scant six inches. It was a foot wide. Three pale pink, ten-inch tall fat candles were spaced the length of the bouquet in fireproof dishes small enough to be concealed and large enough to hold the entire candle if it melted to nothing. I wasn't about to be responsible for ruining Virginia McKnight's white linen with candle wax. Yes, I had outdone myself. Roy McKnight had raised my ire, driving me to a higher level of accomplishment.

"Please say I can take you to chili today." His voice was pleading. He made eating a bowl of soup sound like an event.

I caved.

"Only to chili." I used his phrase, "I'm finishing my delicate job today. I'm in my worst work clothes. If you'd rather, we could postpone until later in the week when I work in front. I'm more presentable then."

"I'm so happy you agreed, I don't care if you go naked, though I don't suppose there's anyway I'd be that lucky."

I could almost hear the smirk I imagined was on his face.

"No, I can guarantee that won't happen. My lunch time is eleven-thirty. I have half an hour. Will that work for you?"

"I'll be there. Bye, Isabelle."

At eleven-twenty-five, the bell over the door tinkled and Roy walked in, all smiles. He was in his shirt sleeves, no tie, and had the sleeves rolled to his elbows. He's dressing himself down for my sake, I thought. I didn't know if I was flattered or insulted.

When I returned to the shop after lunch, a ten-pound box of Brussels chocolates had been delivered. They were ostensibly from his mother according to the thank you card but I suspect Virginia penned the note and Roy selected the chocolates which cost more than the arrangement. With my twenty-twenty hindsight, I know today, Roy would not be outdone. My arrangement was perfect. His chocolates were over the top.

That day began our whirlwind courtship. Roy overwhelmed me from day one. He was the fairy Godmother I'd denied having. He found ways to press expensive gifts upon me.

As a "huge" favor, he compelled me to act as his hostess at a dinner party for some out-of-town customers. He arranged a private fashion show at an exclusive ladies salon featuring gowns with no price tags. He insisted the dress was payment for my services, claiming I had cinched a million-dollar deal for him at the dinner with my charm, beauty and wit.

Talk about gullible! He scattered so much stardust in my eyes I was blinded. I was the Christmas goose being petted while being stuffed full of goodies to fatten me for the kill and that metaphor is the closest description to what actually happened.

We were married a year later. Roy had been pushing for marriage for more than six months but I dragged my feet. I should have sensed there was a problem when I enjoyed my work as much as I enjoyed being with Roy. He wore me down in the end and we had the society wedding he wanted. Mr. and Mrs. Macleroy McKnight posed for the Sunday edition of the Houston Chronicle with our six-tier wedding cake in the foreground.

Roy left at seven am for his office and returned at seven pm. We breakfasted early and dined late.

"This will only be until I have the business solidly launched, baby, then I'm all yours," he would tell me when I said I was lonely.

I began going to the shop after he left for work. If he called, he called my cell. He never asked where I was and I didn't say. I refused a salary but Alice insisted. The first time I had come to work with tears in my eyes, she took me into the back room for a long talk. I admitted that Roy frightened me and had actually shoved me.

"Fine. You needn't take the money. Put it in a can here at the shop. The day may come when you will wish you had something to fall back on. Here, take this card. She's the best divorce lawyer in Houston. I used her. When you've had enough, call her." Alice handed me a business card. I knew Alice was divorced and now I suspicion that her ex was also an abuser.

I disagreed with her assessment of him, Roy was a gentleman who came from a well-to-do home, but I did what she said. My piggy bank can set on top of a flower cooler out of reach. After I cashed each paycheck, I climbed a stepladder and deposited the cash. Roy gave me an outlandish allowance and an unlimited credit card for keeping my wardrobe up-to-date. Most of the allowance was 'canned'.

When he discovered how I spent my days, he was livid.

"How is that going to look to my customers? To my

business associates? To my competitors? They'll think my company is on the rocks when they find you with muddy hands wearing rags for clothes. What are you trying to do? Ruin me?"

He shoved me into the bedroom and slammed the door on me.

"You can stay there until you come to your senses," he ranted at me through the door.

I packed a small bag and left the apartment after he fell into a drunken sleep on the sofa in his home office.

I moved home again when he agreed to allow me to work. He plied me with jewelry and sweet words and promises to be good to me. The clincher that swayed me to return was I believed myself to be pregnant. My periods had stopped. Now I had a responsibility. Having grown up without parents made me feel more keenly how much a child needed a home with a mother *and* a father. I was learning to be more cautious when it came to Roy and because I was, I didn't tell him my suspicion.

Having 'canned' money as a safety net somehow gave me more patience with him. The idea of a child, of Roy as a father, gave him an importance to me. The image softened his sarcasm and gentled his rough handling of me during lovemaking. Roy was very dominant at those times. His treatment skated close to cruelty. I pushed myself to be loving and malleable but he seemed to prefer my coolness and became excited if I thwarted his advances. He forced himself on me at those times and seemed to enjoy them more than usual.

The warning signs were blinking at me in bright neon colors. I began taking a piece of jewelry with me everyday to drop into the can.

He was drunk the night he beat me unconscious. When I roused, I lay on the floor in our bedroom. He was passed out on the bed. I packed a bag, put the rest of my jewelry into my purse and called a cab from the phone in the kitchen to take me to the emergency room. After I was patched together, I went to the police station and filed charges. They took photos as evidence. From the police, I went from bank to bank by cab withdrawing the maximum each time until I had drawn as much as was in the household account. When the debit card went dry, too, I used my credit card and drew several thousand more. By daybreak, I had fifteen thousand in cash stuffed into my handbag. I found an all night diner, had breakfast and called Janet Cole, the attorney whose card Alice had given me.

Janet knew Roy. She was disappointed that I didn't want to strip him clean. We had a long talk and came to an agreement. We would not settle for less than one million dollars cash plus her attorney fees which I expect she doubled for Roy.

Roy fought dirty and he fought tooth and nail but my demands were so modest in light of his assets that the judge granted me all I asked for, my jewelry and the cash.

Roy blocked my way out of the courtroom the day our decree came down. His face was purple with rage.

"You'll never spend that money, I'll see you dead first. You know I can do it."

"I heard that," said Janet. "I'm going from here to the police station to file a report. We have a restraining order on you, don't forget or I'll see you are locked up for contempt."

"You're next, bitch." Roy spat the words in her face before he spun and charged out of the courtroom.

The next sharp turn pitched me face down onto the floor of the car. I heard metal rattle and everything was dark. I pushed myself up to squat on my feet.

"We're in a garage. You're getting out here. I'm going to drive out the back door, across the alley into a car wash and come out the other side shortly. If they find me, they will only find me and a clean car. You're leaving the city in a wrecker. Good luck."

"Right."

The car door opened and a man holding a flashlight helped me climb out. I could see another fellow was unloading my luggage. He hit the trunk with his palm after he closed the lid. An overhead door raised and Janet drove out. The door shut. A light came on and I saw the huge wrecker. My bags were lifted in and stowed behind the seat. I was boosted up into the cab. A man climbed a ladder on the side of the cab and settled into the driver's seat.

"I'm Matt. I'll be your driver today," he said, and smiled at his joke.

"Makes you feel like King Kong, doesn't it?" He bounced on the seat.

I laughed at him. He was funny.

"Yes, it's grand. And big!"

"Let's get underway. Lay down in the seat until I'm sure we have a clean get-away," he told me.

"You sound like you've done this before," I said, and fell sideways. Daylight followed the rumble of a garage door opening. The engine roared, a powerful sound. He shifted into gear and we rolled into sunshine.

I glanced at my watch.

Fifteen minutes later, Matt said, "The coast is clear. You can sit up and enjoy the view."

We were on the expressway exiting the city heading west. Matt drove me to a small town seventy-five miles out of Houston. There was a bus station at a convenience store. He went in and bought me a ticket to College Station.

"When you get there buy a ticket to Waco. You'll blend in with the college kids. From Waco, go anywhere you choose. Don't go to any place you and your ex-husband ever went together or even discussed. Don't go where you have relatives. Do not contact relatives or friends. Understand?"

"Yes, I know."

Janet had covered all of this with me. She used this network which helps battered women escape their tormentors. The network existed because the founder's mother was killed by an abusive husband. The murderer was a stepfather to the man who established the network. There had been no one to give his mother a hand, to help her hide.

"Janet told me the rules. I'll be careful and I will follow the rules. Thank you for helping a stranger."

"My pleasure. Let's get your bags down. Here comes the bus."

I climbed aboard and sat two seats behind the driver, The ride to College Station was not long. I pulled down the baseball cap before I stepped up to the counter where there were cameras and bought the ticket to Waco. I'd spend the night there and decide where I was going to spend the rest of my life.

A cab ride across Waco was a red herring I drew across my trail. I checked into a motel near the airport for the night. There was a dining room where I had dinner. I had no desire to leave the motel to explore.

Earlier when Janet was plotting my escape for me, she handed me a Texas map.

"You may want to pick a new home in Texas. You may want to pick a home in a new state but here's a map, just in case. I hope we can meet again when the coast is clear."

"When will that be?" I asked in my ignorance.

"When Roy McKnight is dead," she said, simply.

The stay at the airport motel was a ruse to make Roy's henchmen believe I'd taken a plane if he put someone on my trail. In the morning, I'd take the shuttle to the airport where I'd get a cab to the bus station and buy a ticket to somewhere.

When I returned to my room after dinner, I spread the map on the bed. After a long deliberation, I settled on Littsburg, Texas, as my new home. I would not go there tomorrow. I would take my time maybe several weeks or months and a circuitous route to get there. In the meantime, I would research Littsburg, make sure I wanted to live there. Libraries were good places to research. Most have computers for public use. I'd use them.

While I was doing my cloak and dagger approach to my new home, I'd get used to my new name. I'm not Isabelle Palmer anymore. My name is Iris Pennington, same initials. I have a new driver's license, social security card, and passport. Janet concocted my new self while we fought for my freedom in court. She has connections with the U. S. Marshal Service and persuaded them to issue me a new identity.

I gazed into the motel bathroom mirror.

"Hello, Iris Pennington."

Three

Over the next months I traveled the state of Texas staying a week or two in a town before I moved on. I crisscrossed the state avoiding the cities where Roy had clients. He'd introduced me to many of them during the time we'd been dating and married; I dared not risk a chance meeting. For the same reason, I avoided vacation resort areas such as the seashore and large cities with tourist attractions.

My hair grew. The weight of the added length pulled the curls lax and they waved around my face. The sun bleached streaks into the already warm brown matching my hair to my hazel and gold-flecked eyes. I spent a lot of my days walking. It was good exercise, didn't draw attention to me and I could afford it.

"Lioness," I said to my reflection in yet another motel mirror as I gazed at the tawny hair and eyes against my tanned skin. I was not pregnant, a big relief. Apparently, I was in such a state—nerve-wise that my hormones had quit functioning. Once I was free of Roy, my body relaxed somewhat and I was my old self.

Janet insisted Roy bring cash money for my settlement and her fees to the final hearing. She went so far as to make it a condition of the settlement. Roy was very much opposed to the idea but his attorney convinced him that not doing so would only cost him more in the end. Janet made it clear that if he didn't agree and bring the money, we would begin proceedings again and this time, we would go for broke, that is, to make him broke. Roy would lose much more of his empire. Texas is a community property state. We could not have sued for half his worth, he'd keep the assets he had before we married but I'd get half of his earnings for the year we were married. It would have given me in excess of five million dollars. He saved four million by cooperating.

"We're going to the bank in the morning," said Janet, after Roy's attorney pulled him away from us. She had counted the money which Roy's attorney handed to her under the scrutiny of the presiding judge.

"These are consecutively numbered bills. He can trace you very easily if you spend one of these."

Janet was right. They would be easily traced.

"Come to my office at nine. I'll get things set up in the meantime."

We parted ways. She to the police station where she intended to file a report on the threat Roy had made in the courtroom and me to my hotel room. I was accompanied by an armed security guard Janet hired. He would be with me until such time as I left Houston.

We met the next morning. She was carrying the briefcase of money and an empty valise. We rode to the bank in a hired car. The bank was expecting us. The bills Roy gave me were exchanged for others. We used the valise Janet brought with her. The car dropped my guard and me at the hotel.

Janet called later. She was laughing

"There was a homing device secreted in the briefcase," she said. "I had my investigator take it apart. Roy doesn't play nice."

Her people smuggled my luggage out of the hotel and delivered it to her office. The next day I went to her office, she smuggled me out and my adventure had begun.

The bus pulled into Littsburg at one o'clock in the afternoon. Through research I'd learned the west Texas town, population 4000, had two motels, a bed and breakfast and a rooming house. I called the rooming house and booked a room for a week and said it could be longer. The owner/operator, a Mrs. Fillmore, said, "No problem." I asked about cabs. There were none. She asked when I would arrive and promised she would meet my bus.

A tall, spindly woman with grey hair arranged in a bun stood in the shade of the hotel awning when the bus stopped. I glanced at my watch. We were on time.

"Iris?" The woman stepped forward.

"Yes, Mrs. Fillmore?" I accepted the hand offered by the bus driver to help me down. I carried my valise of cash. My two suitcases were in the storage compartment.

"That's me. Do you have luggage?" She seemed grim.

I hope I haven't made a mistake in choosing her establishment for a temporary home.

"I do have two suitcases. Are you parked close?"

"I didn't drive. I brought my wagon." She nodded at a red Radio Flyer setting near the curb.

"It's only a couple of blocks. You can stretch your legs."

"Good idea. The bus is roomy but it feels good to get out and stand up."

"You been traveling long?"

"A few weeks, Ive been touring by bus."

"Most folks fly these days. We don't have an airport."

She balanced the two large suitcases on the wagon, one on the rim at the front, the other propped on the rim at the back. I carried the valise.

"I'm afraid of flying." I told the first of many lies I would tell her as I created myself.

"I can pull the wagon."

"It's fine. I'm used to pulling it. Are you ready?"

"Yes," I laughed, "this is fun."

A dusty beat-up pickup nosed into the curb behind the bus. A scrawny leather-faced man climbed out of it. He stared at me or the wagon.

"Afternoon, Evelyn" He tipped a disreputable Stetson at us.

"Afternoon, Bull," answered Mrs. Fillmore, nodding her head in his direction.

I glanced over my shoulder. The fellow was picking up something that had come in on the bus. The driver was holding it out but the fellow was staring after us. I'd have thought he'd be accustomed to seeing Mrs. Fillmore's wagon.

When we were out of earshot, I asked, "Bull?"

"Yes, it's a nickname," she explained unnecessarily, "his name is Jeremiah Jackson. Some folks call him Jem. Most call him Bull."

"Why?" Several unattractive reasons popped into my head.

"His classmates began calling him Bullfrog when the song was popular, you know the one, Jeremiah was a bullfrog."

"Joy to the World is the name of the song, that's the first line, Jeremiah was a bullfrog," I told her. "They don't call him bullfrog anymore?"

"He beat the tar out of anyone who called him bullfrog. He don't mind Bull."

We walked two blocks and turned left for one more.

"He lives here in town?" I was filling the silence. I didn't give a hoot about Bull.

"Lives a couple miles out. Farms, has cattle," she said. "He don't talk much. He's the county's most in-eligible bachelor." She tittered a skinny laugh.

"In-eligible? I don't believe I've ever heard of one of those." I joined in her laughter.

"He never gives a woman a second glance or the time of day. Here we are."

She turned up a drive bordered by a white picket fence. A large two-story house set in the middle of a neatly mowed lawn edged with a flower border. The house and grounds were well-kept but shabby. The house needed paint and the borders were skimpy. Somehow, I need to persuade Mrs. Fillmore to let me be her gardener.

That was another thing Janet and I discussed.

"Do not take a job in the field of horticulture. That's where Roy will expect to find you. You should give it some time before you buy anything in your name—a house or a car. Public records are easily searched and used as a first resource by private investigators, bounty hunters and such. I expect Roy will put a price on your head. Maybe a big one. It could even be for the million dollars he had to give you. We did what we could to protect your new identity but be vigilant and patient."

If Janet had intended to frighten me, she had. I was afraid to breathe.

The boarding house was tidy on the inside. The furnishings were old but in good condition. Mrs. Fillmore gave me my choice of rooms and after touring upstairs, I chose the one downstairs with a door opening onto the wide veranda and the bumped out bay window.

"That's my most expensive room," she told me, "ground floor, private bath and the big window."

"I can see why. It's a lovely room. I don't mind paying

more for it at all. I expect to pay more for the private bath, too. How much are the rooms upstairs?" I had seen four rooms up there and they shared a single bathroom. The rooms were sizable but couldn't compare to the one I had chosen.

"They're thirty-five a week. I figured five dollars a night."

"How about one hundred a week for the downstairs room with the bath? Is that enough? Does that include my meals? Let's make it one-fifty a week with the meals. That's a reasonable amount to me. Will that suit you?" We stood in the front hall with my luggage setting on the floor between us.

She blushed red and a quick expression of relief flitted over her face. I wondered if I had arrived in the nick of time to save Mrs. Fillmore from financial disaster.

"That seems overly generous," she said, in protest.

I could see need battling pride in her eyes.

"What does the Bed and Breakfast here in town charge per night?" I sought to put her conscience at rest.

"Seventy-five or one hundred, depends on the room," she said, and that realization relaxed her somewhat.

"So, I'm getting a real bargain," I told her. "If you decide I need to pay more, I have no problem doing so."

"You sound as though you mean to be here for awhile."

"I may make Littsburg my home. I'm going to try it out anyway," I said, and laughed. I reached into my purse for my wallet and counted out one hundred and fifty dollars.

"Here you are, my first week's rent."

"Your key is in the door." She accepted the money. "Let me know if you need more hangars."

"Thank you."

I moved my luggage into the room and set about making

it my home. A room next to the bedroom had been divided into walk-in closets and bathrooms. A closet and bath connected to my room and down the hall, the bath and closet that backed mine opened to Mrs. Fillmore's bedroom. A large eat-in kitchen, a dining room and a large living room filled the rest of the downstairs.

I opened the door onto the porch and scooted the calico cat doorstop over to keep it open and let fresh air flow through the Victorian-style screen door. I stepped out to admire the lawn and check the view from my little porch area. This needs a rocking chair, maybe two of them, I decided in case Mrs. Fillmore wants to join me. I would ask her if she minded if I bought some chairs.

My room had a big brass bed covered with a rose and white handmade quilt. The rug over the wide plank floor was tones of sage green and pale pink. It looked old, worn and soft. The floorboards around the perimeter of the carpet were stained dark matching the floors in the rest of the house. The bed set against the hall wall and opposite the bed was a fireplace on an outside wall. A large comfortable overstuffed chair set close by. A table draped with a huge doily set beside the chair. I loved my new home already.

When I finished unpacking, I went in search of Mrs. Fillmore. She was in the kitchen.

"May I come in?" I tapped on the door jamb with my knuckles.

She turned from the stove.

"Yes, come in. Would you like a cup of tea? Coffee? Are you unpacked?"

"Coffee or tea would be good. If you don't have coffee made, I'll have tea. Yes, I'm unpacked. Is there a laundromat in town?"

"There is but you may use mine. It's there." She pointed to a door across the room.

"There's a clothes line in the back yard if you have things you don't like to put in the dryer. Cream?" She set a cup of coffee in front of me, poured herself one and joined me at the table.

"I love my room. The bed is an antique, isn't it?"

"It was my grandparent's bed. They built the house. I grew up here." She sipped her coffee and drew circles with her finger on the red and white-checked oilcloth that covered the kitchen table.

"What do you like for breakfast? Ham, bacon or sausage?"

"What do you usually have?" I tried my coffee. It was good and strong.

"I have oatmeal but you need a proper meal with what you're paying."

"I like oatmeal. Let's have that. At lunch I usually have a sandwich, maybe peanut butter and jam or egg salad. I like fried egg sandwiches very much. I'm not a big eater or a fussy one, either." I smiled across at her.

"I can see. You're very slim."

Slim was a nicer way of describing my form. Roy had always said I was skinny.

"What or who are you hiding from, Iris?"

Chapter Four

Evelyn Fillmore peered across the table at me with sharp, blue eyes.

"I'm nobody's fool," she said.

I stared at her. My mouth may have been gaping open. She surprised me, caught me off guard. I could see that nothing I could come up with was going to pass her built-in lie detector. Her attitude reminded me of a very strict foster parent I'd had once.

"I'll tell you but only if I can be certain you will not repeat what I say. My life could depend on your silence. I am not a criminal of any sort, Evelyn, if I may call you that." I returned her gaze with no shame or guile in my countenance.

"Yes, call me Evelyn. You have an honest face. I tend to believe you but I have to be able to sleep at night. Please tell me. I will let your secret die with me. If it is something I cannot live with, I'll ask you to leave." She drew her hands close to circle her coffee cup with them.

"I am on the run, hiding out, you could say. I was married to an abusive man. When he beat me until I was unconscious, I left him and sued for divorce. He was quite wealthy. I have money from the divorce which is how I am able to pay you. Iris Pennington is not the name I was born with but I cannot reveal my true name." I took a deep breath. Evelyn remained stoic. Her expression did not change. I went on.

"My husband was very angry that I left him and he is vengeful. He vowed to kill me the last time we were in the same room which was the courtroom when our divorce was finalized. I'm hiding from him. Do you want me to pack up and leave?"

"My husband was a tyrant, too. He never beat me, just made me miserable from morning to night. Fortunately, I was left this home by my parents and a small inheritance with it. My husband drank himself to death twenty years ago. We needn't discuss husbands ever again." She smiled at me. Her face lit and changed when she smiled. She was a nice-looking woman. I guessed her to be in her fifties, the upper end of the fifties.

I held my hand across to her.

"Hello Evelyn. It's a pleasure and to tell you the truth, a relief to not have to lie to you." We shook hands for the second time.

"Do you really like oatmeal?" She peered into my face as though she expected me to change my mind.

"I do. I missed lunch. Could I have some toast or a sandwich?" My stomach was gnawing at my backbone.

She jumped up.

"Want an egg sandwich? I could go for one. I didn't eat because I wanted to be on time to meet your bus."

"I would love an egg sandwich."

"We'll ruin our dinner but we'll have soup. Do you like soup?"

"I do."

"Go get your laundry. There's a basket by the washer you can use. You can get that started while I make our sandwiches." She banged a skillet onto the stove and headed to the fridge for eggs.

I got the basket and went to my room. By the time the washer filled and I added my clothes, the sandwiches were on the table.

"I have some leftover potato salad from yesterday. I split it between us," she said.

I ate ravenously. I hadn't been this relaxed in what seemed like forever.

"I'll clean up. You see to your things." Evelyn rose and cleared the table.

I put my lingerie in the basket and carried it out the kitchen door to the clothesline. There were more scantily filled flower beds in the back yard as well as a large garden with neat rows of plants poking up through the soil. A walk of stones led from the back porch to a detached garage. I went exploring and peeked inside. A car covered with a canvas sheet set in the two-car garage. The other side was filled with lawn and garden equipment. My inner gardener sparked in excitement when I saw the gardening supplies and the dirt beds in the yard.

I peeked beneath the canvas and saw an old model Ford. Not ancient, but more than twenty years old, I thought. I was bubbling when I went back inside.

"What's with the car in the garage?"

Evelyn was chopping vegetables and tossing them into a pot on the stove that had steam rising from it.

"I'm making chicken vegetable soup for our dinner. The car needs a new fuel pump. I can't afford to buy one and have it put in."

"How much will it cost to do that?" I slid onto a chair at the table.

"The pump is sixty dollars. The labor about the same. Taxes were due. I had to choose. I couldn't do both." She brushed her hands on her apron and gave me a that's-how-it-is shrug.

"Let's talk, Evelyn. I think we are in positions that we can help each other. Come and sit. I want to ask some favors of you."

She was doubtful, I could see by her face, she didn't quite trust me. She sat.

"Before I married, I worked in a flower shop. I've been to college and I have a degree in horticulture. I love to garden—I live to garden," I said, laughing at the joy the very thought of getting my hands dirty gave me.

"My problem is, I cannot get a job doing any sort of gardening. Doing so would only help my ex-husband find me. Please let me take over your lawn and your garden. You will prevent me from going stir crazy. In return, I'll foot the repair bill for the car. We need some wheels."

"That doesn't sound right. You're doing all the giving and paying." She was balking, her pride was ruffled.

"You're giving me sanctuary, Evelyn, and safety. I cannot put a price on my life. By giving me your lawn and garden to care for, you are saving my sanity. It may seem a lop-sided deal to you, I think it is too, only in my favor. Can we be partners? You inside and me outside? Please?"

"You really mean it, don't you?" She stared in disbelief at me.

"I do. Working with growing things is like eating with me. I have to do it to survive." I let my feelings show for the first time in months.

"For goodness sakes, don't cry. Okay, okay, I believe you. I don't know how I can repay you, Iris, but when I find a way, I don't want to hear a word out of you. Understood?" She nearly shouted the ultimatum.

"I understand and I understand." And, I did. No one likes to accept help of the kind I was offering.

She showed me around the yard and put names to the rows in the garden. I didn't tell her I knew what everything was already. I was excited. I could barely get through the evening and had a terrible time falling asleep. I left my bedroom door open to the porch and latched the hook and eye on the screen. The sound of crickets and an occasional bullfrog put me to sleep eventually. I thought of the man, Bullfrog, as I lay waiting for sleep. He seemed a very distant sort of person.

Chirping birds wakened me. The alarm clock on my bedside table showed it was six am. I rolled out of bed, showered and pulled on some overalls and a tee shirt beneath them. I added a long-sleeve light flannel shirt against the chill of the morning air.

I crept quietly out of my room heading to the back of the house but Evelyn was already in the kitchen and coffee was perking on the stove.

"Ah, another early riser," said Evelyn, "good morning."

"It is, isn't it? I'm very happy. I had a terrible time going to sleep. I have a million questions for you."

"Pour yourself some coffee. Shall I start the oatmeal?"

"Sure."

She ran water into a pan without measuring. I got coffee and walked out the back door, down the steps, over to the garden. I saw how I could squeeze in more rows and even more later on as some crops like the early peas died off and I could replant with fall root vegetables. I must have lapsed into a trance because next thing I knew, Evelyn was calling me from the porch.

"It's ready."

I hurried in and took my place at the table.

"Is there a Farmer's Market in town?"

"Yes. It opens in April and goes until the end of October."

We were in March now.

"Is there a plant nursery?"

"Yes, but there's a better one in Barnes, ten miles down the road."

She buttered toast and brought to the table. Two slices for her and two for me. I grabbed one.

"That won't do us any good until the car is fixed. How could I get there now?"

"I can call Bull. He gives me a ride when I need one.

She spread strawberry jam on her toast and offered me the jar. I declined.

"Do you think he would take us? To Barnes to the nursery? He would be perfect with his truck," I said, thinking of how much I could pile into the back of the pickup. I was excited. Joy rose inside of me. Plants were family to me, inanimate beings that replaced the human family I never had. I'd been without my 'family' since I'd gone on the run from Roy.

"I'll call and ask. When did you want to go? What day?"

She took a bite of oatmeal. Hers was plain. I used sugar and milk on mine.

"Today or as soon as he can," I told her. "Is he as grouchy as he looks?"

I wasn't sure I wanted to ride with him.

"Sullen is what he is, not grouchy. Bull never has much to say." She corrected me.

"Did you grow up with him?" Maybe they had been classmates, I thought.

"I used to babysit him." She stopped eating and gazed into the past.

"His parents loved to dance. They would go to a dance every Saturday night. I stayed with Bull. He was a baby, I was sixteen and, my parents said, too young to go dancing." She smiled dreamily at the memory.

"Somehow, I thought he was older. I guess that's why I thought he was grumpy."

I finished my cereal and enjoyed my other slice of toast with jam and my coffee.

"I'll call him." She dialed on the old phone on the kitchen wall. No cell phone for her. I listened to her explain about me, her new boarder and my desire to go to the nursery in Barnes.

When she hung up, she told me, "He'll be here at eight-thirty. He said to tell you to be ready; he doesn't want to wait." She laughed.

"I didn't tell him you were ready right now."

The kitchen clock said seven.

"You're going too, aren't you?"

"No, not today. I'll call Carl to come get the car and I have my church meeting this morning. You'll be fine with Bull."

She rose and carried our dishes to the sink beneath the window overlooking the back yard.

I hurried to my room, stuffed my wallet into the front pocket of my bib overalls and got a notebook and pen from my purse. After some thought, I hung the handles of the satchel of money on a hangar, covered the hangar with a bulky sweater coat, slid the hangar to the end of the closet rod and pushed my clothes toward that end for further camouflage. I have to rent a safety deposit box and stash the cash.

I went to the garage and took stock of the tools and garden equipment. There was a old reel mower. That's what she was using to mow the lawn. The tools looked dull. I made a note on my pad, hardware store, sharpening stone. I walked around the perimeter of the yard gaging the space I had available. By the time eight-thirty came and the old truck stopped in front of the gate to pick me up, I had a list three pages long.

I'd added a straw hat to my outfit and loosely braided my hair into a single braid that hung down my back. I could have walked out of a Norman Rockwell painting. I went around to the passenger side and opened the door to climb in.

"Where's Evelyn?" His voice was deep and what else, bull-frog-y.

I looked into his face. Black heavy brows were nearly covered by his Stetson, he had it pushed so low. I don't believe he shaved this morning, his beard was black and looked thick against his tanned face. His eyes glittered a brilliant blue in spite of being under the shadow of the hat brim.

"She's not coming." I climbed onto the seat and fastened my seat belt. "I'm Iris."

He stared ahead, blinked a couple of times and put the truck in gear.

"The hell you say," he muttered.

We rolled slowly away.

Chapter Five

I opted to ignore his comment and tried to start a conversation.

"So, you've known Evelyn your whole life." I gazed sideways to study him. His plaid shirt sleeves were rolled to his elbows exposing sinewy, brown arms covered with thick, black hair culminating in broad hands that gripped the steering wheel at ten to two.

"Yep."

He braked at a stop sign, lifted a foot to press the clutch, and reached for the gear shift rising from the floor between us. His hand brushed my leg from mid-thigh to my knee as he pushed into second then down again to third, brushing my thigh a second time in the opposite direction.

"Whoops," I said, and tried to scoot to my right but the seat belt held me firmly. I couldn't budge.

"I'm sorry. The belt is tight." I fussed with it, trying to get some slack.

"Nothing wrong with the belt. The truck is old, seat is narrow. If it bothers you to be touched, I can take you home or you can ride in the back." He glanced at me. His face was non-committal. The choice was clearly mine.

"I didn't mean to insinuate that you were feeling me up, I was trying to get out of your way, that's all. There's no need for you to be offended. Shift away."

"I have to."

I was a bit miffed by his abrupt, cavalier attitude. We rode the ten miles to Barnes in silence. He drove straight to the nursery and parked.

"Are you in a hurry? I'd like to look around."

"No rush."

"Thanks." I couldn't help it, I was happy, I smiled at him. His eyes seemed to open wider, surprise maybe? He may have expected me to pout. I learned a long time ago that pouting only made a bad situation worse.

I filled the back of his truck. I had plants and bag after bag of potting soil. I chose half a dozen large ceramic pots in a beautiful, brilliant blue. The young man working in the nursery pulled a cart filled with bags of soil and the pots. I was pulling a cart filled with plants.

Bull got out as we approached his truck. Before he could say or do anything, I lowered the tailgate and vaulted into the back.

"Give me the pots first, please," I told the fellow.

He handed them up to me one at a time.

"Two bags of soil please."

He tossed them into the bed of the truck. I used the bags to line the back of the cab and scooted the pots against them, stacking them in twos.

"Two more bags please." I lined the sides. "Now hand me the pots of roses" I continued loading and arranging.

Bull leaned on the side of the bed, pushed the brim of his Stetson up and watched. I met his eyes a time or two and imagined he was amused. I had to hold a flat of plants on my lap and another between my feet when we left the greenhouse.

"Is there a hardware store here?"

He was preparing to pull out of the parking lot onto the highway. He stared at me.

"Where are you going to put whatever it is that you want?"

I believe he was dumbfounded.

"Between your teeth?" He kept on at me.

"You got me," I said, joking at him. "I only want a sharpening stone. If you were nice, you could carry it in your shirt pocket for me."

He shook his head and drove to the hardware store.

"It will save time if I go for the stone. You won't have to re-arrange the cargo. What size?" He opened his door.

"Small. I'm going to sharpen garden tools, shovels, hoes, clippers and the like," I told him. "Thank you."

He strode off into the store without acknowledging what I'd said. I took in the baggy seat of his well-worn jeans. His boots were very scuffed I couldn't guess what color they'd been originally. Was he destitute? Should I offer to pay him for the ride? Why hadn't I thought to ask Evelyn how much to pay him? I leaned forward over the flat of flowers in my lap and inhaled the spicy scent of dianthus.

He didn't say a word when he came back. He got in, started the truck and backed out of the parking space. I could see the top of the stone sticking up from his shirt pocket. There was a can of oil, too.

I smiled at his thoughtfulness.

"Done?" He asked when he'd rubbed my leg during a shift. I lifted the flat of flowers for a moment out of his way. I left my leg firmly situated so he rubbed it down and up.

"Yes."

When we cleared town he continued to drive at a slow speed.

"Are you having trouble with your truck?"

"Nope."

He was exasperating. His company was tiring. His silence wore heavily.

I persisted, trying to make an inroad into him.

"You're driving slow. I thought maybe something was wrong with your vehicle."

"I'm trying not to blow the petals off of your roses," he said, to the windshield.

"That is sweet. Thank you. Don't you love flowers?" That got me a disgusted glare. Well, a disgusted glare is something—more than I'd gotten so far from him.

We finally arrived back at the boarding house. The drive home had taken half an hour.

"Back or front?"

I assumed he meant did I want to unload in the front yard or in the back.

"Back, please."

He pulled around and parked at the garage.

"Hold on." He climbed out of the truck.

Good grief, the man said something, right out of the blue. He came around to my side, opened the door and picked the flowers up from the floor. He set them on the hood and came back to take the flat from my lap. He didn't move from the door. He set the tray on the roof and reached across to unfasten my seat belt. His near hand rested on my shoulder and the seat back while he reached over me with his right to pop the button on the belt.

His dirty hat brim brushed over my hair, my chin scraped against his scratchy, whiskery cheek.

I raised my left hand to stroke the right side of his face.

"You need to meet Gillette."

"Do I?"

He turned his head to meet my eyes with his and in doing so, his cheek drew across my chin a second time. The contact was superficial. The effect was deep and sharp.

Oh my! His eyes were piercing. They didn't look at me. He looked through me, What did he see?

"Come on. Let's get unloaded." He stepped back, clearing the way for me to get out of the truck.

I grabbed the two flats of plants, carried them through the garage and set them on the lawn. He was behind me carrying two more. We stacked the soil in the garage out of Evelyn's way. I was ready to climb into the back for the bags, pots and plants out of our reach when he took hold of me with both hands on my waist and tossed me into the back of the truck like one of the bags of dirt. I landed on some bags on my hands and knees.

"Ooh," I said, surprised at my sudden flight.

"Oh hell, I didn't know you weighed nothing. You okay? I'm sorry."

"I'm good. Thanks." I pushed myself up from all fours and looked down at him. I have seen the face of a man saying sorry for being physical with me, Roy's face, filled with malice, loomed in my mind. Bull's face was drawn in concern and regret.

"Are you sure? Why don't you sit in the cab and let me take care of this?" He held up his hands intending to lift me down.

"I really am just fine. Thanks for the lift up." I held out my overalls at my hips to show him how much bigger the pants are than I am.

"See, it's my fault, I'm not big enough for my britches." I laughed at revamping the old adage.

"Okay, if you say so. Pass that stuff down."

We emptied the back of the truck. He was going to leave. I have to settle up with him for his time and the gas.

"What do I owe you?" I pulled off my work gloves, stuffed them into an overall pocket and got out my wallet.

His back was to me. He stiffened and turned slowly to face me.

"What?"

"I want to pay you for your time and gasoline. You have no idea how much I appreciate you taking me. I'd like to go again in a day or two if you are free."

"I'll check my f***ing schedule," he said, in a terse voice through clenched teeth. He got in and revved his motor before he tore down the alleyway.

I stared after him in astonishment. He swore at me!

Evelyn walked out of the garage carrying a tray that held three glasses of iced tea.

"Where did Bull go in such a rush? Is something wrong?"

"Yes, I guess so but I don't know what," I told her. "I was trying to pay him and he swore at me and drove off." I reached for a glass of tea.

"Thanks," I said, saluting her with the glass.

"You're welcome. You insulted him. That's the problem."

"He's insulted that I offered him money? You'd think he'd be grateful. He could use a new hat and some boots. Besides, I did owe him, I wasn't expecting a stranger to do me such a favor. I took up his whole morning." I drained half of the glass of tea. I was parched.

"You expected to pay, he expected not to be paid. It was a misunderstanding." She went to sit in a lawn chair in the back yard. I took the one next to hers and saw the paint on them was peeling or gone.

"Let me show you something," I set my tea on the arm of the chair and brought one of the blue pots out of the garage to show her.

"Do you like the color? I can swap them if you don't.

They'll match the shutters."

"It's beautiful. Blue is my favorite and this is a lovely blue." She reached out to rub the smooth ceramic pot.

"Mine, too. What would you think of a blue, white and yellow scheme for the back porch? I want to make us a spot to have our morning coffee."

"I'd like that. What can I do for you though?"

"Make me pancakes with lots of butter and honey instead of syrup for dinner tonight."

"Really? That's what you want?" She was surprised.

"I grew up eating simple foods. They are still my favorite. I couldn't have them after I married. We can afford eggs and meat, I was told." I shrugged my shoulders.

"Please?"

"You win." She sipped her tea. "Carl ordered the fuel pump. He said it would be here in three or four days."

"I was hoping I could get Bull to take me to the greenhouse again in his truck but I suppose that's out of the question now. Where is the shop here in Littsburg?"

"On Main. Go to the corner, turn left and it's four blocks on the right. Hungry? I made ham salad for sandwiches." She stood and put our empty glasses on her small tray.

"I'm starved." We went inside and had lunch.

I made a trip to the bank after lunch emptied the valise and kept only a few hundred dollars. It felt good not to tote that much cash around. I planted everything I had bought this morning and by three in the afternoon I was ready to sharpen tools. The stone and the oil were nowhere to be found. I decided against indulging his bad behavior and went to the kitchen. Evelyn was on the back porch.

"What did you say Bull's name is? I have to call him."

"Jackson, Jeremiah Jackson. His number is 2433. The prefix is 342. We all have the same prefix, the whole town." She hardly looked up from her magazine.

I dialed and waited for him to answer.

"Yeah?"

"Jeremiah?" I asked, as if it could be anyone but him with that voice.

"Yeah. Who is this?"

Croak, croak, went through my mind.

"It's Iris. I'm ready to sharpen tools but I can't find the stone. Where did you put it?"

"I . . .oh hell, it's in my pocket. I forgot to take it out" He sounded disgusted with himself. Not as disgusted with him as I was, I bet.

"You took off in such a hurry, I didn't think about the whetstone until I wanted to use it. Evelyn tells me I insulted you. That wasn't my intention." I tried to sound sorry but I wasn't about to apologize.

"Well, you're a city gal. You wouldn't know we operate on the friends and barter system here."

Jeepers, I was on the phone with Bull and we were having a conversation. He should put a phone in his truck.

"May I come get the stone?"

"Sure." He hung up.

I had expected him to say never mind, he'd bring it to me but he didn't. I went out to the porch.

"I guess I'm going for a walk. Bull forgot to leave something I bought. How far is his place and what direction?"

"To the corner. Go right and it's about two miles. You'll see the mailbox with Jackson on it. Why don't you ride my bike? It's under a tarp in the garage."

She kept her nose in her magazine but I thought I detected a smile on her lips.

"Great. I can get there and back in no time." I hurried to the garage, found the bike and pushed it through the back yard to the front gate.

"See you shortly," I yelled to Evelyn as I passed through.

It's like riding a bike, I laughed, when I remembered how to do it. After a couple of blocks, I was cruising smoothly. I went slow and easy until I passed the city limit sign then I put some muscle to the pedals and seemed to soar along the highway. It was exhilarating. In minutes I slowed for a rundown shack thinking I had arrived at Bull's place. There was no vehicle in the drive. There was no name on the mailbox. I pedaled on. There was another mailbox visible a quarter of a mile down the road. Big trees screened the house on the opposite side from my sight, if there was a house.

Jackson was stenciled in silver peel-off letters on the black mailbox. There was no traffic. I crossed the highway and pedaled up the blacktop drive. This can't be his place. He could buy a truckload of boots for what it cost to pave this drive. When I rounded the screen of trees and shrubs, I saw a low, wide home built of logs with a deep veranda enclosed by railing. The wood was stained dark brown. The lawn was meticulous. A rocker set on the porch near the door of beautiful, leaded glass which conflicted with the rustic style of the house.

The drive continued past and around the porch. I could see part of a huge barn beyond the corner of the house. I got off the bike, set the kickstand and climbed the three steps to the wood porch. I rang the bell and heard its peal inside. I waited. No one came. After ringing three times and waiting several minutes, I heard an engine and followed the porch around in the direction of the noise.

A wide garage set behind the house. One door was open. I recognized the back of Bull's old truck. I took the steps down from the side porch and walked toward the garage. A huge, grey dog, shaggy and unkempt, wandered out of the garage at my approach and stood staring at me.

I've never been around animals. I froze in terror.

"What?"

I heard Bull's gruff voice asking the dog. Next his head appeared in the doorway.

"You must be in an all-fired rush to sharpen stuff. I would've dropped that off my next time in town."

"You didn't offer. I figured you were too angry with me to deliver," I said, risking a poke at him.

"You *were* damn rude," he said, justifying his attitude.

"I set it over here." He disappeared and returned carrying the oil and the stone in his hand.

"You needn't have cursed at me. You could have explained the local custom. Evelyn told me." I stepped closer since the dog wasn't growling. Its tail began to wag.

"And, you can apologize for being rude." He glared from under the brim of his hat.

"Mine was an innocent mistake." I changed tactics. "Do you have time to drive me there again this week? I'd appreciate it."

"I spect you would. What do you have to barter?" Still glaring.

"What would you like?"

His eyes traveled slowly from my face to my feet and to my face.

"I'll think of something."

Chapter Six

My face flushed warm. He was probably sizing me up with an eye to me wrangling cattle or toting bales of hay and not in the sexual connotation that sprang to my mind and sent blood pumping to turn my complexion rosy red.

"I'm stronger than you think." I had to say something. The silence was awkward.

"I tossed you, remember? You don't weigh as much as my dog." The animal knew he was being talked about and went to stand by Bull.

"I'm good with growing things. I can paint . . .things, not pictures." I'd decided to paint Evelyn's lawn chairs while I pedaled out here so I mentioned that skill.

"I'm a good house cleaner if you need housework done. I can scrub floors in exchange for a ride and the use of your truck."

"We'll see. Today is Tuesday. I'll take you Thursday. Same time." He ran an appraising eye over me again and turned slowly to disappear inside the garage. The dog sat in the doorway which I took to mean I shouldn't try to go inside.

"See you Thursday. Thanks again." I called to the darkness beyond the watchdog. The man was just plain unfriendly. That's all there was to it. As long as he was willing to haul me and plants once in a while, his attitude was no problem. At one time I might have been crushed at his abrupt remarks but life with Roy had tempered me. I wasn't nearly as sensitive as I'd been pre-Roy.

I pedaled back to town more sedately. There was a hardware store on Main Street. I stopped and parked the bike in front of the plate glass window where I could keep an eye on it. Inside I went straight to the paint department and selected a blue that would match Evelyn's shutters and the blue pots. I got a quart of paint, a couple of brushes, sandpaper, a scraper and a quart of mineral spirits. Evelyn's bike had saddle-type baskets over the rear tire and a handle bar basket. I divided my purchases between the saddle baskets and pedaled home in excitement.

The rest of the afternoon was spent sharpening tools. I got the hoe, the clippers and the trowel honed to bright metal, sharp edges and oiled after I scrubbed them in a bucket with a brush I found in the garage. Evelyn came to say my pancakes were ready to go on the griddle.

"Come and eat while they're hot." She looked at the tools lying beside me on the lawn.

"They look great. Just as they did when daddy put them away."

"Thank you. Tools last forever if we take care of them. I'm starved, let me put these inside and close the garage door." I stood and gathered the tools. She headed for the house.

I gave the garage a look over as I went to close the big overhead door. Years of disuse showed in the thick coat of dust covering everything. I saw it could use a good cleaning and some organization and just like that, I had a new project. Over pancakes, I got Evelyn's approval to clean the garage and paint the Adirondack chairs on the back porch blue to match the shutters.

"You need to slow down, Iris. You're on the run all day long."

"I know and I love it. I'm afraid to find a job yet. I want to be sure my disappearance worked and I'm truly free of Roy. If I don't have something to do, I'll go crazy. Don't worry, I love doing everything I'm doing," I told her. "It's a good time, too, while the car is in the garage. Do you want to come out and decide what to keep and what to toss?"

"Well, you're the first woman I've ever met who would like to clean out a dirty, messy garage, I can tell you. That place hasn't been cleaned since Daddy died thirty years ago. It's hard to say what you'll find and no, I don't want any part of it. Whatever is there, I've done without for thirty years. I trust your judgment." She refilled her coffee cup and passed the carafe to me.

"It's late in the day for coffee but pancakes taste better with coffee."

"True." I filled my cup.

My night was fretful. I was hyped about my new projects or maybe the coffee kept me awake for a long time—one or the other did. Then, when I did fall asleep, Roy invaded my dreams and I woke in cold fear. Had something wakened me? I lay stiff and absolutely still listening. My door to the porch was open but the screen door was latched. Was someone or something on the porch? For a long while I was afraid to move or relax but good sense finally prevailed, I climbed out of bed and shut the door, locking it. I felt secure and fell asleep.

I kept the door into the front hall from my room open and the sounds of Evelyn stirring in the kitchen woke me. It was six. I stretched, got out of bed and dug my most tattered shorts and shirt out of the dresser drawer. They'd be perfect for the day I had planned. I double tied the laces of my ankle-high work boots and headed for the kitchen and coffee.

"Good morning. Aren't you up early?"

She turned from the stove.

"I am, a little. Is it too late to plant larkspur? Momma always had larkspur in the beds."

"It is late but I'll plant some anyway. If I put it in partial shade where it'll be cooler, I think it will work. Bull is taking me to Barnes tomorrow. I'll check for seed. They may have plants in their annuals. Yes, larkspur would be good." I poured my coffee.

She was stirring our oatmeal.

We ate and I went outside. I decided to clean the garage

first and scrape the chairs if there was any day left when I finished.

I sorted every thing, hauled the good stuff into the back yard through the small door and the junk for garbage pick-up out the big door to stack beside the garbage can in the alley. There was a long workbench on one side of the garage with a big window above it. I would use it for a potting bench. I discovered a rack for hanging tools. I'd planned to buy one at the hardware store my next trip but now I could cross that off my list.

I was dragging several old garden hoses to the junk pile when an approaching engine spooked me. I froze in place until I glanced over my shoulder and saw Bull's old truck. He stopped in the middle of the alley shy of my junk pile and watched me wrestle the heavy hoses onto the heap. When I succeeded, I wiped a dusty arm across my forehead and pulled off one work glove as I moved aside allowing him pull up to the garage.

His window was down. He extended a hand that held my straw hat. I must have left it in his truck yesterday. I took the hat. My fingers brushed his rough, calloused hand. I smiled.

"Thanks. Good morning." I gazed at him. His forehead was visible today, his hat must be pushed back on his head. His face between the dark stubble that covered the bottom half and his equally black brows was browned. Crinkles creased the corners of his eyes in a sun ray pattern. His forehead was smooth and tan. No wrinkles there. Perhaps he's not as old as I think. Sideburns meshed into the stubble, their length identifying them from the whiskers. His full lips looked dry. He looked like he'd been laid beneath the sun to bake like a raisin.

He didn't say a word. His eyes did the head to toe thing and he let his old truck roll on down the alley. I stared after him. I'm going to have a talk with Evelyn about him. He can't be that rude. He must have something wrong with him to explain why he is the way he is, maybe a mental condition.

The slow, deliberate study with those piercing eyes of his

makes me feel naked. The troubling part is that I'm not put off by the feeling. His insolent scrutiny sparks a heat and something violent but at the same time thrilling in me. *That i*s the *really* troubling part—my reaction to him. The response he sparks in me is unique, new to me and not at all unpleasant, quite the opposite actually.

I tied a bandanna across my face leaving only my eyes exposed while I used the push broom to sweep the concrete floor once the walls were cleared and swept down. A big cloud of dust mushroomed out the open overhead door with the final pushes of the wide broom. I leaned the broom against the wall and rushed into the back yard and clean air. I'd go to the house and beg a glass of cold tea while the dust settled.

My body was coated with grey dust. I inspected myself as I crossed the lawn. I was too dirty to go inside. I hope Evelyn is in the kitchen to hear me call.

"My land, Iris, what happened?"

I raised my head. She was sitting on the porch and she had company—Bull was stretched full-length in the other chair. His baggy jean legs culminating in the raw worn boots seemed a mile long. They weren't, he's a bit over six-foot, I'd guesstimate. He seems not much taller than me, I'm five-eight.

"Looks like we're about to be held up," he drawled.

I realized the hanky still covered my nose and mouth and reached behind my head to untie the knot.

"Your money is safe, folks. I'll settle for a glass of tea."

"Here, have my chair. I'll get you some tea," said Evelyn, rising.

"I'll sit on the steps but thanks. I'm a bit dusty."

Evelyn let the screen slam behind her.

"I can hose you down, if you want." He was amused.

"That's a generous and somewhat dubious offer. I believe

I'll decline." I raised my hand to brush back a strand of hair that had fallen over my eye, saw how filthy my hand was and tried to blow the wisp to the side instead.

"Bend over here." He reached and lifted the strand, pushing it behind my ear.

"Better?"

"Yes, thank you. Should I scratch your back?"

He was puzzled.

"The barter biz. Don't I owe you a personal gesture now?" He was fun to poke at because he had no sense of humor.

He glared under half-closed lids down at me on the steps. His glare softened to a superior, lop-sided grin.

"Not with those dirty hands."

Scratch what I thought about the sense of humor, he may have one.

"You going to be clean by tomorrow?"

"I'll look as good as those boots," I told him, jerking my head toward his feet.

He laughed.

I couldn't believe it. I saw a mouthful of straight, sparkling white teeth, dimples in the black scruff at the corners of his mouth and the crinkles at his eyes grew longer. His laugh was deep and soft and made his wide shoulders jiggle.

"They're just broke in," he said, when he recovered.

I was about to argue the point but the screen opened and Evelyn appeared with a giant glass of tea for me.

"You just saved my life," I told her.

"I'm gone." Bull stood and went into the house. He had to have parked out front. He and Evelyn must be close. He is at home in her house. A less familiar guest would have walked around the house instead of through.

"Bye." Evelyn said to his back. "Are you finished in the garage?"

"No. I'm just letting the dust settle. Do you have some rags I can use out there? Something you won't need back?"

"I do. Would you like a sandwich? It is lunchtime. I ate with Bull but I wrapped your sandwich. Shall I bring it?" She got up from her chair.

"Please. Now that you mention lunch, I'm starved. I'll wash my hands out here." I went to the spigot, rinsed my hands, and splashed my face and my arms until they were no longer grey.

"Here's one of those rags for a towel," she said, tossing me a piece of old sheeting.

I dried myself and sat back on the steps. My face and hands were clean but the rest of me was still a dusty mess. She'd made chicken salad, a favorite of mine. I wolfed it down, finished my tea and got to work. The dust had settled. I washed the window and was amazed at the amount of light that shone through the clean glass.

The rack got nailed to the wall and filled with the rake, shovel, hoe, spade and snow shovel. One section of the workbench had a pegboard above. Clippers, screwdrivers, pliers, and the hammer were mounted as I came across them in drawers. There were jars of screws, nails of various sizes and other neat things a handy man would appreciate. I dusted them and arranged them on shelves beside the pegboard.

Beneath the workbench was a shelf its length. A wooden chest was pushed to the back. I pulled the box forward and lifted it to the bench. The hasp was held shut with a padlock. No problem. I'd found a large safety pin strung with small keys in a drawer. One by one I tried the keys until the lock slipped open. The box was full of papers. I moved over a tall, wood stool to perch on and began sorting and reading.

The original property deed was there. The plans for the

house and invoices for the materials were tied together with string. The most curious and exciting find was half a dozen insurance policies. They had been issued at different dates but all more than fifty years ago. The beneficiary was Evelyn Mae Johnson on each.

My first inclination was to run to the house and show them to her. I eyed the box remembering where it had been. Did Evelyn even know about this treasure? Were these policies good? Had they already been cashed? I thumbed through them adding the amounts. Full face value of the six of them would be over two-hundred thousand dollars. They could not have been cashed in, I reasoned, or Evelyn would not be in such dire straits. Were they good? Did insurance policies spoil? No, idiot, they expire or lapse.

I dug into the brown envelope bundled with the policies with a rubber band which had broken when I tried to slip it off. The envelope was filled with canceled checks made out to the various insurance companies. They were neatly arranged in chronological order, the most current payment on top. Mr. Johnson had last paid the premium December 26th, Nineteen Eighty-two. The memo line read 'Premium 1983'.

I wanted to explode with joy but caution ruled me. Tomorrow, I'd talk to Bull and get his recommendation for an attorney to consult. I was excited to think that I could be holding security for Evelyn's future in my hands. I replaced the papers into the chest, locked and stashed it on the shelf.

I put the finishing touches on the cleaning job, dragged the stuff I'd moved to the back yard back into the garage and shut the door down. I cleaned up at the spigot as best I could. I removed my shoes and wiped them with one of the rags. No one was in sight as I peered at the neighboring yards. I stripped to my underwear, left my blouse and shorts outside the kitchen door and made a dash for my room and bathroom.

"Oh my," exclaimed Evelyn, as I ran through the kitchen.

An hour later I joined her. My hair was damp but I was scrubbed clean and felt cool in a cotton sundress with wide straps and a full skirt with flip flops on my feet. We had a nice dinner. She fixed a roast with vegetables roasted in the pan with the beef. I ate like a ditch digger which pleased her.

"When did your parents pass?" I asked as we put the kitchen to rights. She fussed at me, saying I'd worked all day but I enjoyed washing up while she stowed leftovers.

"Momma died several years before daddy. She died in Nineteen Seventy-nine, in the fall of that year, October to be exact. Daddy died the fifteenth of March, the ides of March I always think when I remember that day. The year was Nineteen Eighty-three. It's been nearly thirty years now. Seems like yesterday," she said, wiping the stove top.

"And, your husband?"

"He died the year after Daddy. That would have pleased my father. He never liked Bill."

"That must have made things hard on you, your father not liking him." I emptied the dishwater.

"Not really. By then, I didn't like Bill much either." She laughed.

I did too. I knew exactly what she meant.

That night I had no trouble sleeping and no bad dreams. I dressed in clean overalls and a tee, put on my cleaned work shoes and was watching from the front porch for Bull well before the appointed time of eight-thirty.

I rushed out to get in when he stopped in front of the gate. I was bursting to talk about what I'd found yesterday.

"Good morning. I need a lawyer. Who is the best one in town?"

"Me."

He shifted into gear rubbing down my thigh as he did.

Chapter Seven

"You're an attorney? I thought you farmed and raised cattle."

I ignored the electric tingle in my thigh from the back of his hand as he maneuvered the gearshift.

"I don't actively practice law. I'm licensed. The nursery in Barnes?"

He was at the highway waiting for directions.

"Yes. Well, good that you are one. You know Evelyn, you'll be the best one to handle this for her."

"Handle what? I told you, I don't actively practice. I can't imagine why Evelyn would need an attorney unless it has something to do with you. Who are you anyway?"

"The matter with Evelyn has nothing to do with me except I discovered the situation. Evelyn knows nothing of what I'm about to tell you. I didn't want to raise her hopes in case it comes to nothing." I twisted beneath my seatbelt trying to get face to face with him.

He'd pulled onto the highway and was shifting into third as I squirmed and his hand slid from my knee a good way up the inside of my thigh. Reflex made my thighs close trapping his hand between them and I screamed a small 'eek' in spite of my being clothed in overalls.

He jerked his hand free.

"Calm down. That was your doing, not mine."

"I was trying to turn. Why do you drive this stupid thing anyway?"

I overreacted to the personal interplay which was accidental but had fired a flash of heat that moved as a current through me.

"I admit, this isn't the most comfortable ride in the world. The truck was my dad's. That's why I keep it going. Sorry about the accidental grope."

I changed the subject.

"I found insurance policies insuring Evelyn's father with Evelyn as the beneficiary in a chest in the garage Would they be good after all this time?"

"They could be. It could take forever to research them, to prove they were in good standing when Mr. Johnson died. That's the determining factor, the thing that says they'll pay or they won't pay." He glanced at me.

"Mr. Johnson filed the checks he paid the premiums with in the box with the policies." I squirmed again, trying to make eye contact. I strained against the belt.

"Damn it, sit still. That belt is not elastic. Are you sure about this? About the policies?"

"He wrote premium checks the twenty-sixth of December, Nineteen Eighty-two. He died the fifteenth of March the next year." I was getting excited. I couldn't help it.

"What do you think?"

"I don't think, I prefer to know. I hope *you* know what you're talking about. She could use a break. You saved her temporarily when you came and insisted on overpaying her."

His jaw was set as though he was angry. He couldn't be angry with me, I hadn't done anything wrong. I struck out at him.

"Couldn't you have helped her? The two of you seem to be friends," I said to him because I really wondered why he'd let her be hard up when he seemed comfortable financially.

"Are you in the habit of accepting money from friends?" He turned to flash angry eyes at me. If he hadn't been mad before, he certainly was now.

"No." I muttered.

"Neither is Evelyn."

He was speeding. It felt like he was driving too fast.

"You're very judgmental," I said, as though I was unaware that he was put out with me.

"Says the woman who accuses me of ignoring a friend in need," he said, through gritted teeth.

"You know, you're very free with the insults and curses for someone who's so quick to take offense," I answered his thrust with a parry.

"You're opinionated and you way overuse that adjective, very." He snorted.

"You sound like a bull, Bull."

Suddenly, the absurdity of our conversation hit me and I burst into laughter. My hand reached over and slapped him gently on his leg and stayed to squeeze before I realized what I was doing and let go. I looked at him. He couldn't hold his composure and he joined me. I laughed until I had tears in my eyes.

When I finally stopped and wiped my eyes, I told him, "Darn that felt good. It's been ages since I've had a good laugh."

"Why?"

"It's one of those long stories with a bad ending. You should thank me for not telling you," I kept my eyes on the highway. A sympathetic look from him would have been my undoing this morning. I was restless but didn't know why. I feared I was having a premonition of bad things to come which could only be Roy.

"Bad divorce?" He asked quietly.

"Amen." I whispered.

"Is it over and done with?"

I nodded my head. I couldn't speak. It *was* over and done with but I hovered out of sight hiding from the specter of Roy or his hireling. Would it be this way the rest of my life? That's the part that wears and tears at me, the fear that he'll never give up and go away.

"You're hiding." It was a statement, not a question.

I nodded yes.

"I expect he thought you said very too much, too," said Bull.

I laughed again, by myself this time. I glanced at him when he didn't join me. His jaw was set in a grim line.

We were there. He pulled in, and parked.

"Remember, every thing has to fit in the truck."

"Right."

I transformed when I entered the nursery grounds. My troubles blew away in the gentle morning breeze. I grabbed hold of one of the handy wagons for shopper's use. I felt him against my side.

"I'll do that," Bull said, taking the wagon handle from my hand, "you need both hands to grab stuff."

I screwed my head around to smile at him.

He looked away, deliberately avoiding my eyes.

Our earlier exchange had made me think that he and I were going to be friends now. I should have known better. He is incorrigible. He has a friend in Evelyn and apparently he needs only one. I'm wasting my time cultivating him.

Each time I filled the wagon, he came with an empty one. Finally, he said to me, "We only have room for three more flats or however many pots fit that space plus what you want to hold on your lap."

We had been there for nearly two hours I saw when I

checked my watch and bent backward to stretch. I'd been bending over tables of perennials for a long time.

"Already?"

"Yep."

I sighed and selected three more flats, a gallon of Buddleja to sit between my feet and I stood staring at two yellow rose bushes, fidgeting, trying to decide which I could hold like a mother choosing between her children.

Bull saw my dilemma.

"You can set one pot on the seat between us."

I gleefully put both buckets in the wagon.

"Thank you. I needed both."

"Spect so." He pulled the wagon toward the checkout desk.

I followed behind giving him the once over, like he does me. His shoulders are broad beneath the faded work shirt that was tan when new. He is slim, I'd say scrawny but I think men prefer wiry to scrawny. His clothing fits loosely—baggy is more accurate. His disreputable hat is usually pushed down shielding his face from view. He doesn't own a razor, I guess, or hates to shave though he doesn't have whiskers, just stubble. His boots are . . .well, I've seen better on a homeless tramp. I've studied his hands as he drives. They are broad and, I know from touching them, calloused and strong. His nails are cut blunt and are clean. Maybe he does have some redeeming qualities. I've eyeballed him before and make him to be half a head taller than me, not like Roy, who towered above me menacingly.

When we got to the truck, I was amazed at how much I'd bought. I went back to pay while Bull supervised the last bit of loading. Either he or the nurseryman had devised a way to stack the flats in the back of the truck without damaging the plants. They'd inserted shelves with legs between the layers. I had bought a shameful amount. Evelyn would be overcome. I couldn't let her see them all at once. I'd have to sneak them into her garden a few flats at a time.

Bull didn't speak the whole way home. Neither did I. I would have been talking to myself. When we drove into town, I broke the silence.

"Would you drive around to the garage? I don't want Evelyn to see all of this and worry. I didn't realize what I was doing. You should have said something."

"I did. I told you, three more flats." He was serious.

I sighed in frustration and he heard.

"Don't take that tone with me. I only pulled the wagon."

He helped me unload. I set flats around the yard where I wanted to transplant them. Some I carried to the front. After they were scattered, they were not as imposing. The buckets I set on the lawn by the garage. Some would go into the blue pots.

"That it?" Bull stood, hands on his hips, ready to leave.

"Got time to look at the policies? Maybe you could take them home with you to study."

"Get 'em."

I squatted to pull the chest from the back of the shelf. The glass in the window made a cracking noise. The next thing, Bull was on the floor beside me.

"Son of a bitch! That was a shot. Someone is shooting this way."

My eyes rolled up in my head. I fainted.

He was shaking me.

"Iris, are you hit? Are you hit? Damn it, Iris, answer me."

I surfaced. My eyes opened. Bull was holding me by my shoulders. My head lay on his knee as he squatted beside the workbench.

"I don't know," I whispered. "Can you see him? Can you see Roy?"

"Who the hell is Roy?"

"Oh my God, Evelyn! Is Evelyn all right?" I pushed against him, struggling to get to my feet.

"Dammit, Iris. Stay down. Who is Roy?"

"Ex-husband. I have to find Evelyn." I could feel tears building as I pictured her lying on the kitchen floor in a pool of blood.

"Don't move!" He ordered. He was dialing his cell. I listened as he explained our situation to the 911 operator. He slipped his cell into his shirt pocket and there was nothing more to distract him, he had to look into my face.

"Let's check you. I don't see any blood. That's good." He rolled me around and over in his arms checking for a wound. He was strong. He handled me as if I was a rag doll.

"I think you're fine," he pronounced.

We heard sirens.

"Let's move away from the windows before we stand up." He duck-walked with me in his arms to a corner out of sight of the windows and stood. He let my feet drop to the floor and kept his arms tightly around me. We were beside a small window that looked into the back yard. He moved to glance at the house.

"Evelyn is okay. I see her on the porch. She's wondering about the sirens."

My legs started shaking. I slipped my arms around his chest and let my body lean against him. He felt me collapse and tightened his arms to hold me upright.

"You're going to be safe," he said, squeezing me, his chin resting on top of my head on his chest.

A sheriff's car stopped behind his truck in the alley and a tall uniformed man walked through the open overhead door.

"What's going on, Bull?" His glance swept over us in the corner and back to the window.

I looked at it too. There was a bullet hole in the glass.

"Alvin, say hello to Iris. She is Evelyn's boarder. She has a story to tell, I think, but she's shaking out of her boots at the moment. Maybe we can move inside and sit her down first." He stooped, slid one arm behind my knees, swooped me into his arms and carried me toward the house.

Evelyn saw us coming and got excited thinking I'd been hurt and wondering why the sheriff was in her backyard. By now, I was shaking uncontrollably, too much to be able to speak.

"Where's her room?" Bull asked Evelyn.

"The downstairs front." She stood aside to let us pass. The sheriff stayed in the kitchen with Evelyn.

Bull kicked the door shut behind us with his foot. He dropped my feet to the floor and encompassed me with his long arms, shushing me and massaging me from fanny to neck with his broad, hard hands. My forehead rested against his cheek. I nuzzled into his neck with my nose and sighed. We stood like that forever but I think forever was less than ten minutes. He waited a couple more minutes after I quit shaking before he stood me on my own feet and peered into my eyes.

"Gonna make it now?"

"Yes. I'm better. I need to pack. I have to get out of town. I don't know how but he has found me." I stared up into his eyes. They were kind. How had I not noticed that about them?

"I think I know how he found you." He reached into his shirt pocket for a folded sheet of paper he handed me. "I took it off of the wall behind the cash register at the nursery."

My picture was on the poster.

"Reward for information," it read. "Missing, believed to be suffering from amnesia." The poster went on to say that I had wandered out of a hospital where I was being treated following an auto accident. The reward was twenty-five thousand dollars.

My eyes rolled up in my head. I felt his arms tighten around me.

Chapter Eight

This time I fought the urge to swoon and grasped his shirt keep my balance.

"He knew a nursery would be the place I'd be spotted. Janet warned me to stay away from the business but I didn't think he would go this far to find me." I shuddered as I imagined Roy's face.

"He really loves you, huh? Doesn't want to let you go?"

"I expect he hates me because I got away. Roy is cruel, Bull. I left because he beat me badly."

"Roy . . .would that be Roy, as in Roy McKnight?" His hands held my shoulders and he bent to meet my eyes with his.

I nodded yes.

"I'm Isabelle McKnight. I took the name Iris Pennington when I escaped."

"Escaped?"

"He wants to kill me. I sued him for a divorce and a million dollars. He told me I'd never get to spend the money the last time I saw him as we left the courtroom. My attorney got me a new identity and sneaked me out of town in a giant tow truck."

Bull threw back his head and laughed.

"There's more to you than I thought, Iris Isabelle."

"It isn't funny, Bull. He's scarier than the devil. He is the Devil." I shuddered violently.

"I know. I'm laughing at you, you've got some moxie." He gave me a tight hug.

"Look at your door. Is it supposed to be like that?"

I turned in his arms to see the door. The screen had been

slit and curled back onto itself so someone could reach inside and unhook the latch. I gasped.

"That's a no, huh? I wonder when that was done."

"It wasn't like that when I left this morning."

He looked around.

"Someone has searched your room."

I'd left the inner door open that morning and the screen door latched.

The suitcases I'd stored beneath the bed were pulled out, laid open on the floor and compartments split with a knife or other sharp instrument. For some reason, a box cutter came to my mind and I imagined if I'd been sleeping and he'd come through the screen and cut my throat like he'd done the screen.

"Let's check your closet," said Bull, steering me that direction.

My clothes were on the floor or hanging skewed from bent hangars. The valise was on the shelf. It was empty. I knew that. The money and the jewelry were tucked safely into safety deposit boxes at the local bank. I'd had to rent three of their largest boxes to hold the contents of the valise. I'd split the cash into three bags which I fit into the baskets on Evelyn's bicycle the day after Bull took me to Barnes the first time. The jewelry was stuffed into a tote bag I wore over my head and one shoulder.

"Are you up to talking to Alvin? He's the sheriff."

"Yes." My voice was trembling, I was shaky but somehow, I'd come to the conclusion that I was done running.

"It's time to take a stand, isn't it?" I looked into Bull's eyes.

"Atta Girl." He patted me on the back and opened the bedroom door.

Evelyn had made coffee. She jumped up and poured me a cup when we walked into the kitchen. Alvin was at the table with coffee and a plate of cookies in front of him.

"I'm going to the garage while you two talk. You'll need to take a look at her room before you leave, Alvin. Is there a key I need, Iris?"

Bull was antsy. I guess he wants to get away from the shooting and the histrionics.

"Yes," I answered. "On the safety pin in the drawer."

"I should have known that. I'll be back in a bit." He walked out the back door shaking his head and chuckling.

I knew he was going to get the insurance policies from the chest. I crossed my fingers that he was going to find a boon for Evelyn.

"Tell me your story, Iris," said Sheriff Smoats. "It appears we have a killer in our midst. We tend to frown on people who do that sort of thing around here."

"I married Roy, Macleroy is his name, McKnight two years ago. He began shoving me, then slapping and finally beating me with his fists when I displeased him. You see, Roy was well-to-do and a socialite. I grew up in the foster care system. I'm not sophisticated. I didn't need to do much to displease him. I liked to work and I had a job with a florist shop. That's how we met. I delivered flowers to his office.

After he beat me so badly I had to go to the emergency room, I didn't return to our apartment, I hired an attorney and sued for divorce. We had been married six months. The divorce took more than a year. He fought it. He begged me to come home but I knew he only wanted to hurt me for leaving him. When I wouldn't give in and go back to him, he became vicious. Roy told me I would never spend the money he was ordered to pay as our settlement. I was given a new identity and new documents. My attorney worked with the U S Marshall service to get me new identification.

I stayed on the run for months then came to Littsburg to

settle and live."

I handed over the poster from my lap beneath the table.

"Bull saw this on the wall at the nursery in Barnes. We should ask if they contacted that number," I held up the poster, "to collect the reward. Bull drove me home, we were in the garage. I bent to pick up something and the shot came through the window. If I hadn't stooped, I may have been hit."

"Oh Iris," moaned Evelyn, wiping her eyes on the corner of her apron.

"Someone broke into my room, Evelyn. They cut the screen to unlatch the hook. I left the door open this morning and latched the screen. I'm sorry." I reached over to pat her hand.

"Oh my." She got up from the table and disappeared down the hall to check the damage.

"I need the address for your ex-husband, please," said Alvin. He had produced a small notebook from a pocket and flipped it open.

I gave him Roy's office address as well as the apartment in the Washington Towers.

"I'm stepping out to call my deputies. Be back in a minute," said Alvin.

He went to the back porch. I could hear him instructing them to sweep the town for a Harris County license plate. He and Evelyn returned at the same moment.

"Have you been to the nursery here in town? Maybe they called for the reward." Alvin took his chair at the table and reached for a cookie. "Any coffee left, Evelyn?"

"No, I haven't been there. I went to the hardware store. I've ridden Evelyn's bicycle through town. I try to stay out of sight as much as possible and not do anything to draw attention to myself."

"You've done a pretty good job. I haven't heard a word

about a new person in town. Do you have any idea what you'll do now?"

"I have to move. I don't want to leave town though, Sheriff. I can't stay here and put Evelyn in danger."

The stark reality of my situation was beginning to creep into me. I felt chilled in spite of the heat of the sunny spring day. I sipped my coffee and held the cup to warm my hands.

"What about the Sommers' place, Alvin? It's fairly defensible. Not too many ways inside." Bull had come in the back door. He sat down between Evelyn and me.

"Have you ever seen these?" He laid the insurance policies on the table in front of her.

She picked up the top one and read enough to get the gist of it, put it down and picked up another. One by one she scanned them before she raised her head to stare in shock at Bull.

"Are these real?"

"They are real. I'm ninety-nine percent sure that they are collectible, all of them. May I handle this for you?" Bull was pleased. His pleasure showed in the crinkles around his eyes and the slight curl of his lip as if he might smile.

"Where did you get these?" Evelyn was trembling. She picked up a policy for a second look.

"Iris found them in a chest in the garage while she was cleaning out there. She asked me to look at them for you."

She looked from Bull to me, back to Bull, and then me again. Her bottom lip trembled and her face began to crumble as tears overcame her. Bull stood and pulled her up from her chair. He gave her the same treatment I'd gotten from him earlier when he'd calmed me.

"What's the deal?" Alvin was in the dark.

"They are insurance policies her father had on himself and Evelyn is the beneficiary. If they are good, her problems are over," I told him. "How do I find out about the house Bull mentioned? I need to move immediately."

Evelyn heard me.

"You don't need to leave, Iris. We'll be fine."

"Thank you, but I do have to go. What if you had interrupted that fellow when he was searching my room this morning? You could have been killed, Evelyn. I can't endanger you or anyone else with my troubles." I turned to Alvin.

"Where is the house? Who do I see about it? Is it for rent?"

Alvin's cell rang. He rose and dug it out of his shirt pocket as he headed out the back door. He was back almost immediately.

"They caught him. The boys radioed Barnes and they shut down the highway there. He drove right up to them. He's got a rifle in his trunk. I'm betting the slug we dug out of the garage is gonna be a match for his gun. I gotta go, folks. Can you see to her, Bull?" Alvin inclined his head in my direction.

"I reckon," said Bull, his expression saying he'd just been unfairly punished.

I'd had his "put upon" attitude up to here by now. I stood and moved my chair into place.

"If you'll tell me who to contact about that place, I can handle it. There's no need for you to be inconvenienced further." I got the memo pad and pencil Evelyn keeps by the phone to jot down the particulars.

"Who do I see?"

"The Sommers have passed on. Their attorney is handling their estate. You'll need to see him," said Bull.

"Do you know who he is?" That was a silly question. There couldn't be that many attorneys in a small place like Littsburg.

"Yep. Me."

He seemed to derive pleasure in turning my every attempt to escape his domain back to him. At each new juncture I was beholden to him in some way whether it was a ride, advice or the comfort and strength he dished out when I needed some.

"Did you or did you not tell me that you do not actively practice law?" I sounded strained, nearly shrill. My nerves were chafed.

"What he means is, he doesn't charge anyone," said Evelyn. She was recovered.

I couldn't help myself, it all caught up with me. The threat of Roy, the fear from months of running and hiding, the shooting today and this stubborn misfit of a man who thwarts all my attempts to befriend him but stirs a terrible, strong compulsion to be close to him in me. In his way, he was as cruel as Roy. Bull is in no way physically threatening, but he jerks my feelings around as though I'm a yo yo with no control over how he does me. I burst into sobs and ran from the room. I shut my door and locked it. My suitcases were still there on the floor. Alvin had left without coming in to see what had been done here.

I bawled silently, tears ran down my face and dripped off of my chin as I folded clothes into the two damaged bags. When the closet was empty, I went to clear out the bathroom. I ran into Bull as I came out, my arms loaded with toiletries.

He gripped my arms tightly.

"I spect you need to calm down."

I stared up at him through a waterfall of tears.

"I *spect* you need to let go of me. Tell me who to see to rent the house, please, and you'll never have to see me again."

"Me. I told you already, I'm the one. Is your stuff packed? I'll take you there." He was clenching his jaw, the white line between the stubble and his lips gave him away.

"Give me the key, tell me how much and I'll get there

myself," I hissed at him. "How did you get in here? I locked the door."

"You locked one door. Now, let's hit the road. You're upsetting Evelyn."

He flipped the lock on the hall door, picked up my suitcases and walked out leaving me there with my shampoo, toothpaste and bath soap in my arms. The screen door with its mesh cut and folded back explained how he'd gained entrance. The same way my stalker had entered. I followed him to the kitchen.

"Here Iris, let me get you a sack." Evelyn took the bottles from me and handed them back in a plastic bag.

"I'll call you later."

I nodded. I was numb. I'd cried myself out and run my emotional gambit. I was shattered and followed Bull out the door, across the yard to his truck parked in the alley. He tossed my suitcases into the back. I climbed into the passenger seat.

"The Sommers were good people. After he died, she became paranoid. The windows have bars and the doors are impenetrable. You'll be safe. You need to set up deliveries for everything you need so you don't go out until this is over."

He drove in beside a tall stucco fence and stopped.

"The security starts here. The gate is electric and has to be opened from inside once we turn it on."

He reached across me and fished in the glove compartment for a ring of keys. He slipped off several keys, climbed out and used a key to unlock the tall iron gate. I got out clutching the plastic bag and waited for him to tell me what to do. I was beyond acting for myself.

Bull retrieved the two suitcases from the back of the truck and led the way inside to the front courtyard. He set the cases down and turned to me.

"This is a safe area for you to garden. The wall is tall

enough to keep out anyone and there is no place within range for a shooter to climb and be above you. There's not so much as a utility pole he can scale. Let's go in. We'll check the back."

I rotated taking in the courtyard that was outlined in raised beds. Big pots set here and there. Dead plants hung down their sides.

He unlocked the front door. I moved after him and stepped inside. The interior was cool.

"Everything is here, it's completely furnished. All you'll need is groceries and plants." He set my suitcases down and took the bag from me.

"Come with me. Let's see if the back yard is safe. You'll fill the front in no time." He took my hand and pulled me through the house to a kitchen door that had window panes in the top half.

"That is unbreakable glass," he said, unlocking the door. We stepped outside. The back yard was a twin to the front only bigger.

"There are no two story houses for a person to see into the yard," said Bull. "There are no trees big enough to support the weight of a man. I believe you can use both the front and back, Iris."

The gentleness of his voice brought me out of my spell. My trials and tribulations were none of his doing. I was shocked, yes, but now I was being childish and petulant.

"I apologize. I'm sorry for wimping out. You're right. I can be safe here and feel safe. Before I lock myself in, I need to go to the bank for some money. Who knows how long I'll be confined. How do I pay the rent and how much is it?"

"The estate is being settled. The Sommers left the house to me. I don't want rent. You'll be keeping the house in better shape than standing empty would. I'll take you to the bank. You shouldn't be out alone. The utilities are all on including the phone. We'll leave things in the Sommers' name. Alvin, Evelyn and I will know how to reach you so answer the phone if it rings. Ready?" He asked.

I frowned, not knowing what he meant.

"The bank."

"Oh yes, right. Yes I'm ready." My purse was on my shoulder. I dug out the bank box keys on the way and stuffed the purse with cash when we got there. Bull stopped at the grocery after the bank. I filled a cart.

"Only one?" He raised his brows.

"This isn't the nursery," I said, and laughed. The laughter made me feel whole again. I took a deep breath. My world was righting itself.

He helped me carry the groceries inside.

"I have to go but if you'll make a list, I'll go to the nursery in Barnes for you tomorrow or the day after," he told me, as we stood at the front door.

"Really?"

"Yep.

He was back to his old self.

Chapter Nine

I watched through a front window until he was out the gate and hurried to the pantry to turn on the power. The gate could only be opened by me from inside now. There was a button by the front door for operating the gate to let guests enter.

My first task was putting away groceries. Next I toured the house. It was a lovely Spanish-style full of arched doorways. Saltillo tile floors were scattered with a patchwork of luxurious area rugs.

I moved Mrs. Sommers' clothing aside in her closet and hung mine. Mr. Sommers' clothing filled the other walk-in. I stripped the bed and tossed the sheets into the washer. The furnishings were draped with dust covers. One by one I pulled them off, took them out through the double garden doors to the side yard and shook them before I folded them. There was a storage closet in the hall and I stowed them there. The vacuum was in the storage closet. I spent an hour running it through the house and then an hour dusting. Afterward, I vacuumed a second time and the day was gone.

The phone rang. Evelyn was checking on me.

"Have you eaten, dear?"

"Not yet. I have groceries though. I believe I'll have an egg sandwich or an omelet. The house is nice. I like it." That was true, I do like the house.

"I worked on the plants for you. I hope you had them where you wanted them. All of the flats are planted," she said.

"Thank you, Evelyn. I forgot about them. Your yard is going to be gorgeous in a few weeks."

"Good night, dear."

"Good night."

I left the sheets in the washer and found clean ones in a linen closet to make the bed. Tomorrow I'd hang the others outside to dry. I made a peanut butter sandwich and took it and a tablet to bed to start a list for the nursery.

I wakened. The bedside lamp was on. My tablet was on my stomach. Half of the sandwich was on the plate lying beside me on the bed. I hoped I had eaten the other half because I couldn't find it. Not even under the covers. I laid the plate and the tablet on the nightstand, turned off the light and curled up beneath the blanket. Bull's face was the last thing I remember.

I brewed coffee in the old percolator on the stove top. While it perked, I hung the sheets out to dry. I ate two eggs and toast standing at the sink looking out the window. The house was nice, I was safe but I was lonely, so very lonely.

That's what I had enjoyed at Evelyn's, her company. That and the freedom to move around out of doors and work with plants. Up until the time I'd been discovered and shot at, that is. Well, I could work out side and work with plants but I'd have to talk to them, there would be no one else.

The morning was spent cleaning house. I washed windows, mopped floors and scoured both bathrooms. The kitchen got a going over. I took stock of the cupboards and the fridge and made a list for the store. Bull had spoken to the grocer yesterday telling him enough of my situation to get the man to agree to deliver to me. They delivered to shut-ins, Bull had told me, so I was no big stretch. I am a shut-in of sorts.

Bull. He kept popping into my head. If I was at Evelyn's still, I'd pick her brain about that man. If I were out and about, I could ask people but I am in solitary confinement. My first impression of him was that he was none too bright, maybe mentally disabled in some way. I surmised so because he spoke only in monotones and avoided eye contact. Turns out, he's a lawyer

His derelict style of clothing had me believing he was

homeless or near to penniless but I'd seen his lovely home. The fact that he is an educated man of comfortable circumstances makes his behavior all the more weird. To say he is a man of few words would sum him up. Is he shy? There's no such creature as a shy attorney, is there? If push came to shove or in his case, shy came to rude, I'd have to choose rude. I would brush him off, like he deserves sometimes, except I'm developing this horrible yearning for him and his company. I'm thirty-three, rather old to be having a school girl crush. I sighed and made myself a sandwich for lunch.

Bull is not coming today or he would have been here already. After I eat, I'll start cleaning the outside areas. The front first, I think. If I have guests, they'll enter through the courtyard so I'll make it welcoming before I do the back yard. I took my tablet outside with me in case inspiration hit and I needed to add to my nursery list.

There was a glass-topped café table of wrought iron with matching chairs, two wood garden benches, a large, empty, three-tier fountain and half a dozen chairs of wrought iron or wood strewn about the courtyard. The large pots were terra cotta and the built up planters edging the space were plastered with stucco, also terra cotta. Definitely Spanish influence, I thought, and that calls for bougainvillea. Did I want purple or pink? Pink, I decided and added bougainvillea to my list.

The nursery had a nice selection of cacti I'd seen on previous trips. I wrote in the names of several and made a note "large" beside them. I swept the tile before I hosed the dust and all of the furniture down. The colors of the wet decorative tile scattered through the pattern glistened in the sunshine.

There was a door into the garage from the courtyard and I found a wheelbarrow and other lawn and garden tools. They need sharpening. Did no one take proper care of their tools anymore? A whetstone was another note on the shopping list. I found the bucket I wanted and a brush to use on the fountain.

I was standing in foot-deep dirty water scrubbing the

upper tiers of the fountain when the gate opened and Bull stepped inside. My back was to the gate. I heard the creak of the hinge, threw the brush into the air and jumped like I'd been shot because I thought a shot was what I'd hear next. I fell into the dirty water, cracking the side of my head against the bottom tier of the fountain as I went down.

My brain went foggy for a few minutes though I don't think I lost consciousness. I heard Bull swearing in a distant part of my head and was aware of being lifted. I opened one eye and gazed up at him. He looked quite odd, fuzzy around the edges. I reached one hand up to touch his face and missed his head.

"Whoops," I mumbled, "stand still." I tried again and missed him a second time. I gave up, sighed and closed my eyes. I must have passed out because I felt his lips on mine so I was dreaming. They were soft, not dry as I supposed, and very gentle. Too gentle, I wanted more. I reached up and pushed the back of his head to bring him closer, my lips opened beneath his and returned the kiss with a passion I didn't know was in me. I moaned and stroked my hand down the side of his face to hold his jawline in my palm. What a lovely dream. His lips moved away. I sighed. Too bad. Dream that again, I thought to myself.

"Iris," his voice whispered into my face. His breath brushed over my face. Toothpaste. His breath was fresh toothpaste. I licked my lips, he'd tasted like toothpaste, too. Someone should make strawberry toothpaste, I thought, that would make a good kiss.

"Iris," the voice came again, soft and feathery but not strawberry. He cursed and that was neither soft, or feathery and certainly not strawberry.

My eyes popped open. He wasn't quite as fuzzy as before but why three eyes? Two noses? That can't be right. I closed my eyes and opened them again. I was right the first time—two noses. One eye was gone, he only has two now. I shut my eyes not wanting to deal with the problem. Bull looked funny. He'd have to fix it himself, not me.

Sounds, odd sounds surrounded me. They didn't matter, I was sleepy. Bull's voice was one of the sounds, his and another voice. I was chilly but too comfortable to do anything about it, even complain. Opening an eye was out of the question. So was speaking, I could barely listen.

"Overnight, slight concussion, no fracture," were words that penetrated the veil that surrounded me. I felt myself lifted, Bull has me, I know the feel of him. He's carrying me away. To sleep, I think. I'm being lowered. A bed, it's cool and hard.

"No," I force out the word, "hold me."

I'm lifted. It's Bull. I nestle into him and moan when my head brushes against him. He's moving me and then his arms wrap around me. I sigh. This is good. I wake. I sleep. He talks. I hear him.

When I wakened, it took several moments to make sense of my situation. Bull's face was not a foot from mine. Our heads were on a pillow, the same pillow. How did that happen? He was sleeping soundly. His arm lay across my ribs. I was covered. He was not. Bit by bit I was piecing things together. Bull and I were in bed together. Nice. I moved closer and put my arm against his chest, my hand on the side of his neck. He stirred.

"Iris?" he whispered.

"Mmm."

"Iris?"

"Shh." I wiggled closer and stuck my face into his chest. He was warm. I slept and dreamed of soft lips on mine.

I woke again. I was in a bed. Sunshine shone through the slats of venetian blinds. Bull wasn't in bed with me. Another dream, I guess. I moved my head and moaned because it hurt.

"Easy, champ. You took a ten count. Lie still."

I moved my head to connect with the voice. Bull sat in a chair beside the bed.

"Where am I?"

He was sipping coffee. His face was very dark, I wanted to touch his cheek but he was too far from me.

"Hospital. You hit your head when you fell."

I remembered.

"The gate opened. I was afraid it was him coming to kill me."

"Sorry, it was me. I came for your list. I'm sorry," he repeated.

"Can I go home?" I felt naked out in the open. Why did my first coherent thoughts have to be of the danger threatening me? Preservation instinct, I suppose.

"Wait and see what the doc says." He closed his eyes. He did look tired.

"Were you here all night? I dreamed about you. I dreamed I woke up and you were in my bed."

"That was a nightmare, not a dream." He didn't answer me.

I forgot I'd asked.

A young man in a white lab coat entered my room. The stethoscope around his neck hinted he was a physician. "Good morning, Iris. Let's have a look at you this morning. Got a headache?"

"No." I told him.

"Yes, she does," said Bull, from the peanut gallery.

I jerked my head intending to scowl at him and pain shot through my head. I groaned.

"It doesn't pay to lie," said the doc. He shined his light in my eyes. Took my pulse and listened to my heart.

"Do you live alone?"

"Yes."

"Is there someone who can stay with her around the clock?" He spoke to Bull, not me.

"Yep."

Who could that be, I wondered. Evelyn, he must be thinking of her. That would be lovely except what if a killer came? What would Evelyn do? What could Evelyn do?

"I'm going to discharge you, Iris, on the condition that you have a caretaker, twenty-four-seven. I want you on complete bed rest for one week. You may sit in a chair for an hour at a time. It's all right to shower if someone is on standby—by that, I mean close by. I want to see you in my office at the end of the week."

"When can I garden?"

"We'll see. Maybe after a week you can start some light chores outside. You are not to work inside either for this week, understand?" He peered over his half glasses down his nose at me.

"I can fix my meals, can't I?"

"No. Bed rest or sitting in a chair." He was emphatic. "Understand? Can you tell her caretaker to monitor her activities?" He asked Bull.

"Yep."

"The nurse will be here in a few minutes to sign you out. You may get dressed, Iris. See you in a week." He walked out scribbling in my chart as he went.

"Oh. My clothes! What about clothes?" I jerked, felt pain, calmed myself and turned to Bull, who was pushing himself up from his chair.

"Hold on." He picked a bag up from the other bed and brought it to me.

"Beggars, choosers, I just grabbed something to cover

you. I hope that's your robe." He rose and pulled the privacy curtains around my bed. "I shut your door but I'm staying inside. You heard the doc."

"Thank you," I murmured.

There were panties, a bra, nightie, robe and slippers in the sack. I groaned as I sat up, the curtain parted and Bull was in my enclosure. I hurt too much to mind.

"Need help?"

"Yes," I whispered. A whisper was all I could manage. He moved to stand behind me, picked up the bra lying on the bed, untied my hospital gown and pushed it down my arms. Next he held the bra for me to slide my arm into, eased it into position and fastened it. The gown came next. Still from behind me, he held the sleeves for me to put my hands through and pulled the nightie over my head letting it puddle around me on the bed. He came to face me, picked up the panties, slid one leg over each foot and pulled them just past my knees. The slippers went on my feet. He worked my arms into the robe.

"Can you stand a minute?"

"Yes."

He slid me forward off of the bed and pulled up my underwear. The gown and robe were lifted into place and the robe tied shut. Then his arm slid behind my knees and I was lifted back into bed. He pushed the curtains aside.

"Okay?"

"Yes. Thank you."

My head was aching. I felt exhausted. I closed my eyes and listened to the nurse instructing him on my care which sounded like a long list of do s and don't s. I hope she gave him a written list. He'd never remember everything to tell Evelyn. When she finished, Bull lifted me into a wheelchair but not until he warned me.

"Iris, I'm picking you up. Time to go home."

The nurse pushed me to the back exit. The sunlight hurt my eyes. I squinted. The truck setting there was old, but it was not Bull's old truck. The shaggy grey dog was in the back of it. He opened the door and bent to lift me.

"Upsy, here you go." He situated me, and pulled a seat belt across my front.

"Lay your head back. Keep your eyes closed. I should have brought dark glasses." He shut the door gently.

I blessed him for not slamming it.

I tried to ask him a question as he climbed into the driver's seat.

"What?" he asked, leaning to put his ear in front of my lips.

"Your truck?"

"This truck *is* mine. The other one is Dad's. We're in disguise. Can you lay over on me? I don't want people to see you. If you can't, don't worry about it."

I braced myself with one hand on the seat and lowered my head to rest on his leg. He patted my shoulder.

"Good girl." He kept his hand on my shoulder as he drove me home to the Sommers' house.

He used a garage door opener and drove into the garage. Before he unloaded me, he shut down the garage door, unlocked the door leading into the kitchen and checked the house over. The dog went with him.

"I'm taking you inside. Your bed is turned down." He unbuckled me, scooped me into his arms and carried me to the bedroom

"Stand, let's take off your robe."

He stripped the robe away, lifted me into bed and removed the slippers.

"I should have asked. Do you need the bathroom?"

"No, I'm okay. Where's Evelyn?" I sank onto the pillow and my headache eased.

"I don't know. I spect she's at home. I'm going to go lock the garage and show Chester around." He left the room.

Chester, I thought. He must be a male nurse. That's probably better than Evelyn. Taking care of me for a week would be too much for her. I'm glad Bull thought of that.

"We're shut up tighter than Fort Knox." said Bull, coming into the room. "Are you hungry? I can scramble an egg for you."

"What about Chester?" Why wasn't the nurse preparing my meal?

"He's already eaten. Would you like something else? I do a mean flapjack, too."

I could feel his presence near my bed and like a flash flood I burst into tears. Having him here with me was such a relief. My nerves were stretched taut, I was overwrought. His nearness was a balm that broke through my veneer and like a pilgrim reaching home, I broke.

He sat beside me on the bed and gathered me to his chest. His hands rubbed my back, his lips whispered in my ear.

"You're safe, Iris. No one can get to you. Things are going to be fine. Shh, now."

My arms circled his chest. I held on as though I was hugging a life preserver. This uncommunicative, distant, loner had become the most important person in the world to me.

"Shh, be still, relax. You need to stop crying. Tears will make your head hurt. Shh," his lips moved down my jawline, his whiskery cheek scratched my smooth one.

I took a deep breath and shuddered, letting go of the tension that filled me. I loosened my hold and rubbed over his back with the palms of my hands.

"You make me feel safe," I murmured. "I don't know what I'd do without you."

"You won't be. I'll be right here," he whispered, squeezing me tightly to him.

"I thought Chester was going to take care of me," I hiccuped.

"Chester is my dog. I'm your caretaker."

Chapter Ten

"You?" I jerked backward to see into his face.

"Would you rather have a regular nurse?" He dropped his arms from around me.

"It's up to you. I'm more protection than a nurse but a nurse would have a better bedside manner. You think it over and let me know. I'm going to fix something to eat. I haven't had breakfast." He stood.

"I'll have whatever you're having to eat. Thank you for taking care of me. You're the only person who makes me feel safe. Can I come to the kitchen for breakfast?"

"I'll come get you when it's ready." He left.

I lay back against the pillow and contemplated my situation. My small fortress was a prison no matter how nice it is, not that I mind being confined while I have Bull for company. My memory of kissing him in my dream was real enough to stir feelings in me when I relive the moment. Would an actual kiss be that good? There was only one way to find out. I'd make kissing Bull my goal for the day. I closed my eyes. My headache was gone. I was smiling.

"You awake?" He asked softly not wanting to wake me if I wasn't.

My eyes popped open.

"Yes, I am and I'm starved. My head doesn't hurt." I pushed myself up in bed and started to swivel my feet out.

"Hold on."

He came and sat on the bed, lifted my legs and draped them over his lap. One arm went behind me to support my back and the other beneath my knees. He rose taking me with him and carried me to the kitchen. A kitchen chair had been replaced by a small, stuffed armchair. He lowered me gently into it and scooted me closer to the table. For all his rough edges and tough guy act, Bull is surprisingly gentle. I'd say he's a gentle giant except he is regular size.

He had made pancakes, and fried bacon and eggs.

"This is a feast," I told him.

"I buttered those hot off the griddle," he said, indicating the cakes.

I ate two hot cakes, one egg and two strips of bacon.

"I'm going to have to dig today to keep this from going to my hips," I said, with a laugh.

"I don't think so, you heard Doc. Besides, you could stand to put on a pound or two. We could get your planters cleaned out and refilled if you'd like." He glanced my way. I noticed he didn't maintain eye contact.

"How would we do that?"

"There are some boys I know. I'll have them come, dig out the old dirt, empty the big pots and then do whatever you tell them to do." He got up and carried the empty plates to the sink.

"Would that work? More coffee?"

"That would be great. Would it be safe?"

"Yes. I'll be outside watching. You won't be in sight. Is that a yes?" He looked at me, raising his black brows in askance.

"Yes," I whispered. I was moved by his thoughtfulness. I think he is trying to please me, make me happy, keep me safe. I wanted to go hug him.

"Is something wrong? You look funny." His hand gripped the edge of the sink, he stared at me.

I expect he thought he was going to have to rush me to the emergency room again.

"I'm happy."

He rolled his eyes and turned on the water to rinse our plates.

"I would drink another cup of coffee when you finish the dishes." I admired him as I watched while he did what I thought would be unfamiliar chores with the ease of long practice.

"Do you have a housekeeper?"

"Nope."

"Ever been married?"

"Nope."

"Do you want to?"

"Want to what?" He is playing dumb. I know he is.

"Be married."

"Nope."

"Why?"

He stopped working, turned off the water and turned my direction.

"How'd that work for you?"

"I was steam-rolled. I'd love to marry the right man."

"Good for you. Get back on that horse." He finished at the sink, brought the coffee pot to the table and filled our cups.

"Alvin called." He sat down in his chair and set the coffee pot on a trivet.

"Are you up to talking about Roy?"

"Yes."

"The fellow they arrested in Barnes was definitely the shooter. He refuses to say a word but ballistics matched the shell in Evelyn's garage to the gun in the trunk of his car. He lawyered up. He's being held without bail."

"He won't admit Roy hired him?

"Nope. Alvin is pursing another line, though." Bull drummed his fingers on the table. I wanted to reach over, cover them with my hand and stop them but I didn't.

"What?"

"He went to the nursery and visited with the owner. After Alvin explained about becoming an accessory to murder, the fellow opened up and told Alvin everything he knew and everything he had done." Bull grinned, as he recalled Alvin's words.

"Zeke, that's the fellow's name, got the poster a couple of weeks before I took you there the first time. He thought he recognized you even though your hair is different."

"Yes, I let it grow to change my appearance."

"Well, it didn't work. He sneaked a picture of you on his cell while you were shopping and called the number on the poster after we left. Turns out it was an answering service and they would only take a message. Zeke told them he had a picture and left his phone number. He got a call but it was a wrong number. He told them they got the nursery in Barnes by mistake—they thought they were calling a backhoe man, they told him. Zeke didn't realize they played him." Bull chuckled.

"When Alvin clued him in, his lips got really loose."

"What do you mean?"

I pictured the nursery man as I remembered him. He didn't seem dangerous but he had sure enough dumped me into a pit of snakes.

"Zeke was playing it safe. He wasn't about to get cheated out of twenty-five thousand dollars. He recorded the call to the answering service. When he got the call back, he recorded it, too. He figured it was the people calling about you when his cell rang and afterward, he didn't bother erasing the 'wrong number'."

"Is it Roy calling? Is it him on the phone?" My heartbeat doubled.

"Alvin wants you to listen to the tape. He's going to come by in a couple days. In the meantime, the Houston PD is looking into the shooter with an eye to connecting him to Roy. So, things are progressing.

I spect you've been up long enough," he stood.

"I can walk. Just let me lean on you for balance."

He pulled my chair back and I stood keeping hold of the table top. I turned to him and put one arm around his waist.

"Lead on, Mac Duff." I squeezed his hip with my hand. He felt lean and muscular.

"Are *you* feeling *me* up?"

"Yes, I believe I am," I said. "You're very muscular. Do you work out?" I squeezed him a second time.

"You need to stop that. I'm here to protect you, that's all. I could be your father and it's indecent of you to try to tempt me if that's what you're doing."

"How old are you? Evelyn said she babysat you." I rubbed over his hip with my palm erasing the squeezes.

"Never mind my age, I'm old enough to do what I want, you are not."

We had reached the bedroom. I sank down on the side of the bed. He bent to pick up my feet.

"I can do that, but thanks. I don't know how old you think I am but I'm old enough to do what *I* want to do, too."

"Good for you. Find another man. I'm not available." He wheeled around and stalked out of the room.

Talk about touchy! He was pricklier than a porcupine. I lifted my feet into bed and lay back on the pillow.

"So, how old is old enough, to do what you want, in your mind?" He was standing in the doorway leaning against the door jamb. He'd come back.

I sat up.

"I'm thirty-three. I'm divorced. I grew up an orphan. I'm not sixteen hoping to go to the prom. I'm not a twenty-year-old on the prowl. I'm not on the rebound and after your body because I can't live without sex either."

I was heating under his scrutiny. His eyes were smoldering beneath the brim of his hat which I've yet to see him without. Evidently he wasn't there the day boys were taught not to wear their hats inside.

"I'm old enough."

"Why hit on me?" He was relentless.

"I didn't know I was hitting on you. I am, however, attracted to you for some reason that I am unable to explain because you do everything possible to put me off you."

"So, you want me, is that what you're saying?" He crossed his arms and one foot over the other.

"I'm saying yes, maybe I do, in spite of yourself."

I'd let exasperation put words in my mouth and said much more than I intended. More than I knew, really. I am attracted to him in every way, including a desire for intimacy, but I've never dwelt on my feelings beyond kissing which I'd dreamed about. I flopped back on the pillow and closed my eyes wishing I could disappear. When I opened my eyes a minute later, *he* had disappeared. That couldn't have been more embarrassing unless I'd been standing naked in front of him saying those things.

The day passed slowly. I feigned sleep if I thought I heard him coming down the hall. There was a lot of activity. I could hear voices, the door opening and closing and other sounds I could not identify. Several times I sneaked into the bathroom and once I got as far as the kitchen thinking I'd make myself a peanut butter sandwich.

"What the *hell* are you doing?" He shouted at me.

I froze midway across the kitchen.

"I'm hungry. I thought I'd make a sandwich."

His arms came around me from behind, he turned me, his head lowered and he gave me a kiss that stopped my heart and would have made me sink to my knees if he hadn't held me upright.

"You don't have kitchen privileges," he whispered, when his lips let go of mine. He scooped me up and set me in the armchair at the table.

"What would you like?"

"More," I said, giving him a big smile.

"To eat?"

He *didn't* return the smile. The look he gave me made my heart flutter instead. My he can say so much without opening his mouth.

"Did you have lunch?"

"I don't do lunch usually. What were you going to make?"

"Peanut butter sandwich."

He made the sandwich, added an apple to the plate, and poured a glass of milk.

"Eat it all." He set the plate in front of me.

"I'm going outside. I'll be back to take you to your room and you better be sitting right there." He disappeared into the hall. I heard the front door open and voices outside.

I finished eating and drained the glass of milk. He walked in just as I set down the glass and his eyes swept over the table confirming I'd eaten all of my lunch.

"Let's go." He pulled back my chair. "Can you walk?"

"Yes."

He was distant and cold—all business. I must have gone too far. Admit it, I said to myself, you've done everything but yank off his clothes and order him to bed. My goal was accomplished, though. I had kissed him. The kiss was not my doing. He'd kissed me out of the blue and it was every bit as good as in my dream. This is a good place to end our romance that never was, I thought. I was ashamed of myself for pursuing him as I had. My behavior was brazen and that's not me.

"Thanks for the lunch and the escort," I told him, when I was situated sitting on the bed. "What's going on outside? I hear noises and voices."

"It's the guys I told you about. They're digging out the planters and emptying the big planting pots. It's going to take a few days. You should work on your plant list. When the fellows finish, I'll have soil delivered and the planters refilled. What kind of dirt? I need to get the order in."

"A mix of half topsoil and half potting soil. I probably need to go to the bank. I don't think I brought enough money for this big a project."

I swung my legs up onto the bed but didn't cover myself. As soon as he left, I intended to use the bathroom and have a nice hot shower.

"You don't need more money. This is my house and the work has to be done before I can put the house on the market. Consider yourself a consultant. We'll swap your expertise for rent." He started to leave.

"The old barter system at work," I mused aloud to myself.

He heard.

"Yep," he said, without turning.

The front door opened and closed. I hurried into the bathroom, used the toilet, shed my pajamas and hopped into the shower. The water felt wonderful. Gingerly, I worked shampoo into my hair. Only the side I'd fallen on was tender. I lathered and rinsed my entire body. It seemed ages since I'd had a shower instead of two days. I stepped out and wrapped a towel around my body and another around my head.

He caught me at the sink, brushing my teeth.

"I'm starting to feel like a parrot, having to repeat myself. What the hell do you think you are doing?" His face was stern, his hands were on his hips, in angry mode, and his voice several decibels too loud.

My free hand went to my sore head and I squinted at the volume of his voice. The other hand took the brush out of my mouth.

"Brushing my teeth."

He interpreted my squint correctly and whispered, "Get your ass back to bed. Don't you know you could fall? Do I have to sit with you every minute?"

I put down my toothbrush, rinsed my mouth, massaged my hair gently with the towel covering it, then folded the towel over the rack to dry. I turned to stare at him. Tears welled in my eyes.

"No, you don't."

I walked toward him and he stepped aside to let me out of the bathroom I ducked into the closet, closed the door, let the tears fall and slipped into clean pajamas. I ran my fingers through my hair to fluff it, I don't think he'll let me up long enough to dry it. I did dry my eyes on the bath towel and emerged from the closet.

He sat in a chair across the room. His head in his hands and hands on his knees.

I stopped to stand in front of him.

"I wanted to feel clean."

I went to the bed and climbed in. When I shifted, I could see the chair. It was empty. He was gone. I cried myself to sleep.

I woke with a headache. I figured my throbbing head was

brought on by the stress of dealing with Bull. I was going to get up for some aspirin but when I lifted my head from the pillow, a shooting pain made me lie back, close my eyes and try not to breathe heavy. I must have fallen to sleep again.

The next time I woke, I sensed I was not alone.

"Who's there?" I whispered.

I felt the bed sink beside me.

"It's me," said Bull. "How are you feeling? You look pale."

"Not too good. My head hurts. I guess I shouldn't have showered," I admitted he was right.

"No, I should have thought of that. I could have bathed you or called a nurse to come do it. We won't make that mistake again, okay? I'm sorry I'm not much good at this nurse business."

He reached over to feel my forehead. His hand was rough and warm. I raised mine to grasp hold of his.

"You're doing fine. I hate using your time this way. I'm sure you have other things to do. Maybe I should hire a nurse for a few days," I said, giving his hand a weak squeeze. The movement caused a spasm of pain and I gasped, wrinkling my forehead in reaction to the sharp stab in my head.

"I'm calling Doc to come by. This isn't right for you to hurt this way. Can I get you anything?"

Yes, I wanted to scream at him. Hold me, hug me, tell me I'm safe, tell me everything is going to be okay.

"No, I don't need anything," I lied to him. "Maybe the doctor is a good idea."

I felt him rise from the bed. I hadn't opened my eyes during our exchange of words. I thought he had left the room. I let go of the feelings I held inside and tears rolled out the corners of my eyes onto the pillow. I tried to relax. Deep breath in and slowly let it go, I coached. Free yourself, relax, float away on a cloud. I tried every technique I'd taught myself from the age of five up. Five was the earliest I could remember. Dream of a fairy, a fairy mother, that was my five-year-old coping mechanism. Surprisingly, the method still worked. I concentrated, made myself go limp and transported myself to a dream world not too different from "The Land of Oz".

My scarecrow resembled Bull. The tin man had Bull's face. The Lion had his face and his disposition. I drifted to sleep unaware of Bull watching me from the chair a few feet away.

Chapter Eleven

Their voices were low, they didn't waken me. I lay with my eyes closed and listened as Bull discussed me with another man. The other voice must be the doctor's.

"Should she be hospitalized?" asked Bull. "She wouldn't like this known but she's had a tough row to hoe and she's done it all by herself."

"Her physical condition is great. I should be in such good shape. She is in better condition than many athletes. Has something happened to stress her? Stress could cause her to be tense. Tension can cause her to have a headache."

"Hell yes, she's under stress. She's under a shit load of stress. She divorced her husband because he beat her and now the son of a bitch is trying to kill her *because* she divorced him. He has the same as put out a wanted, dead or alive, poster on her. Twenty-five thousand dollars, that's the reward he's offering to anyone who tells him where to find her. A guy from Barnes called the ex-husband, told him she was around here. She was shot at a few days ago. Luckily, she moved at the right moment and the shooter missed. She's staying here because it's easier to protect her with eight-foot walls surrounding the place.

Can she be up and around? A little maybe? How about taking a shower? Would that be all right? How long can she be up, sitting in a chair, I mean. If she can do more, maybe she won't be as tense. You know, take her mind off her troubles a little. What do you think?"

That has to be the longest speech Bull has ever given, The urge to smile made me twitch. Bull must be looking at my face because he spoke to me immediately.

"Are you awake, Iris? How do you feel? Can you open your eyes? Doc is here."

Bull is going to be worn to a frazzle from all this talking.

I forced my eyes open, a gargantuan effort. They must be swollen from all of the crying I've done lately. I seem to cry at the drop of a hat or on the hour. Maybe the doctor is right and it's stress. Bull is right, too. The idea of Roy hunting me down like a wild animal to kill me makes my blood run cold and keeps me looking over my shoulder. I'm afraid to close my eyes or to relax into a deep, restful sleep.

"Yes, I'm awake. I can't seem to keep my eyes open though." I cracked one eye open. Bull was sitting on the bed beside my hips. The doc was in the chair.

"We're discussing your stress level, Iris. Do you think medication would help you to relax? Your head injury shouldn't be causing you this much discomfort. There was no sign of a fracture and no swelling. The injury could be where your stress is manifesting itself though. You know, nerves can make us have muscle tics, blink a lot and even stutter." Doc spoke from his chair.

I turned on my side to face him.

"No, no tranquilizers. I need to be alert. I've cried a gallon of tears today. That's my body letting out the stress, I think. I'm going to be fine. I need to get up and be busy. That would help." I pushed myself to a sitting position. No pain!

"Okay, you win. You can get up and move around the house. After two days, if there's not another headache, you can work outside. No heavy lifting. Boss around those fellows Bull has out there. I'm going to leave a sleeping pill for tonight. Take it. A good night's rest is better than a dozen pills."

He rose and stooped to pick up his medical bag sitting beside the chair.

"Call if you need me. Take care, Iris, and keep your head down." He smiled at me and walked out.

Bull followed Doc down the hall. I heard them at the

door then Bull came back to me. I closed my eyes.

When next I wakened, the house was quiet. The faint sounds of voices and digging were gone. The house was filled with a wonderful aroma of something good to eat. I was immediately hungry. My head didn't hurt. I felt heavy, my head weighed a ton. A crying hangover, I told myself, no more crying. I lifted my head to sit up and Bull stirred. He was stretched long in the stuffed easy chair across from the bed.

"You're awake."

"So are you. What am I smelling?" I swung my legs to dangle over the side of the bed.

"Dinner. Bathroom?" He stood and came to help me.

"Yes, but I think I can manage."

"I'll walk you in and wait outside." He put his hands on my waist and lifted me upright.

I wavered which made him think I wasn't steady on my feet but it was his nearness that affected me, not my concussed condition. He tightened his grip when he felt me tremble.

"See, you do need help."

My nose was tickled by his chest hair exposed by the two top buttons open on his shirt. I grabbed hold of his forearms for balance.

"I've been lying around too long. I need to get up and move." I tried to cover my reaction to him.

"Okay. We'll take you to the kitchen when you're done in the bathroom. You can watch while I finish dinner. Come on," he turned me in the right direction, held onto the arm closest to him and kept his free arm around my waist.

"You'll have to let me plant a big garden for you to make up for all I owe you. Is there a limit to how much I can owe on the barter system?" I rambled as we crossed the room to the bathroom door. He left me as soon as I had the vanity to hold onto and pulled the door closed behind him. I used the toilet, brushed my teeth, combed my hair and reached for the door as he pushed it open.

"What's taking so long? Are you all right? It's been a long time." He blocked the doorway. One hand extended to me and he gently pulled me close. His eyes searched my face with intense scrutiny. What was he looking for? Signs of pain? The wobblies? Surely not for the adoration that was plastered all over my face.

"Is something wrong?"

He didn't answer. He turned us and we walked to the kitchen together. After I was planted in my chair at the table, he switched on the radio and began puttering.

"Could I help?" I knew the answer before I asked.

"Can you cook?" He was lifting a small roaster out of the oven. He set the pan on top of the stove and flipped his hand violently. "Damn it all!"

I jumped up and hurried to take his hand.

"What happened?"

"Burned my hand. That damn thing is too thin." He scowled at the hot pad he'd tossed and flipped his hand again.

I got an ice cube from the freezer and rubbed it lightly over the red welt forming a blister on his palm.

The Oldies radio station played softly and Charlie Rich came on singing, Behind Closed Doors. Bull took the ice cube from my fingers, threw it across the room into the sink, took me in his arms and floated me around the kitchen in smooth, gliding turns.

"No," I whispered into the side of his neck. My heart was fluttering. My stomach quivered.

"No, what?" he murmured, against my temple.

I could feel his voice though my lips against his throat.

"I don't cook," I muttered.

He was strong, I could feel his strength. My one hand crept across his shoulder and the other up the arm holding it until my fingers laced together on the back of his neck. His hands lowered to my waist and rested on my hips. I leaned into him and sighed in utter contentment. He radiated warmth through the thin fabric of his worn, faded shirt. He must have a closet filled with worn-out shirts. His body felt solid and sturdy, not the least bit wiry or bony and he smelled of the soap I'd placed in the bathrooms.

When the music stopped, we stood in our embrace. I didn't want to move. Why Bull didn't move, I don't know but finally he stepped back, keeping his hold on me.

"Go sit."

He turned me away from him and went to the cupboard for plates. He laid silverware on top and brought them to the table.

I leaned against the back of the over stuffed chair and closed my eyes hoping out of sight out of mind really worked. My body reacted strongly to him, making me heady. The sensation was new, strange and put me in an emotional turmoil. Dealing with him while my head was not on straight from the fall was too much. I need to insulate myself against him, not let him get to me every time we got within six feet of one another.

"Alvin is coming by in the morning. He'll bring the recording Zeke made of the phone call. Maybe you'll recognize Roy's voice. Of course, that doesn't prove anything."

"What do you mean it doesn't prove anything?" I opened my eyes and stared at him.

"Him calling there, especially when he pretended he reached the wrong number only proves he made a phone call. It is however, a brick we can use to build a wall of evidence against him."

Bull lifted the roast onto a platter and spooned the vegetables from the roaster onto the platter with the meat. He ran water into the roaster, squirted in dish soap, and carried the platter to the table. "Sorry, I didn't get a salad made," he said, as he sat down opposite me.

"It looks and smells wonderful."

He cut a serving from the roast, put it on a plate, added vegetables and handed it to me.

"I didn't make dessert either," he said, with a grimace.

"Thank you. I've already confessed that I don't cook. This is terrific. Don't apologize." I cut off a bite of roast and popped it into my mouth.

"Mmm. Wonderful."

He filled a plate for himself and placed the platter between us on the table. He tried the roast.

"It is good, isn't it?"

"Yes. Did your mother teach you to dance?"

He was a long time answering me and sighed before he did.

"Evelyn told you." he said, "Yes, my mother did teach me to dance. What else did Evelyn tell you?" He lifted his eyes from his plate to gaze across the table at me.

"She only said your parents loved to dance and she used to babysit you when they went dancing. I supposed your mother taught you."

I tried a bite of potato. He'd cooked an onion, potatoes and carrots with the roast. The potatoes were small, new red potatoes which always seem to taste sweeter than baking potatoes. The baby carrots were tender and sweet, too.

"Is that all she said?"

"No. She said you are the town's most ineligible bachelor.

What did she mean by that? Are you the victim of a bad relationship, too?"

"I used to date. The women invariably tried to change me —usually my wardrobe."

I laughed.

"That explains your well-worn jeans, shirts and scruffy boots."

"Scruffy?" He tried to appear offended but nearly smiled.

"Yes, scruffy. I thought you were down, out and homeless the first time I rode to Barnes with you. That's why I offered to pay you. I thought you needed the money, you know, for new boots." I was smiling.

"The joke was on me after I saw your home."

"You were just like the others. You told me I needed to get a razor," he recalled.

"A lady doesn't like to get her face scratched but *your* whiskers are very masculine and sexy. By all means, keep them. Maybe you'll find another woman who appreciates them."

"Thanks for your permission. I'm not in the market to find a woman. Does that mean you are giving up on me?" He shifted his gaze back to his plate.

"Yes, I am. I would not dare buck the town's authority by tampering with its most ineligible bachelor. There's probably a hefty fine for messing with you." I laughed. "Are you a local landmark?"

"There's no need to make fun of me." He gave me a wry grin. "Why did you marry him?"

His question hit me like a bucket of ice water. I went from laughing to leery.

"I don't know. I think it was easier than fending him off any longer. Roy is very compelling. He is relentless. He overwhelmed me with his wealth. He showered me with gifts constantly. I'd always been poor or on the verge of poor. I was easy to impress. He convinced me that I loved him. I believe I was in awe, not in love."

I stared at my plate, embarrassed at having to admit to Bull how stupid I'd been.

"I was ignorant. I'd grown up without affection or love. I didn't know how either felt, love or affection. That's how naïve, I was." I gazed at his face expecting him to be disgusted by my confession.

"He should be horsewhipped," Bull said, in a steely voice with his face in a scowl dark as a thunderhead.

"There is no fine for messing with me, though," he said, with a devilish grin. "You could consider me a challenge."

"Is there a prize if I win the challenge?" My voice dropped to a whisper.

"Yeah. Me." He bored into me with an intense look.

"I've learned my lesson. I'm going to have to take a long, hard look at you. I'll have to study you and know you're safe. I cannot be hurt again." I tried to seem as though I was teasing though my words were true. His quasi invite to 'pursue him' made my heart beat faster.

"Ah, you don't trust me."

"It's not that so much as you've made it clear that any interest I may have had in you is not reciprocated. That's the same situation I had with Roy. I did not return his love if that's what that was, and it didn't work." I shrugged my shoulders, trying to seem nonchalant.

"I don't want that again."

"That's part of the challenge, changing my mind, making me reciprocate." He wasn't grinning at me now.

Chapter Twelve

I had to lower my eyes. His gaze was too intimate, too intrusive. I felt exposed. My cheeks flamed with heat.

"Would you like me to help you do the dishes?" I changed the subject.

"No. I'll help you back to bed unless you want to sit up for awhile." His demeanor was back to normal—noncommittal and impersonal.

"I think I'd like to go to my room," I told him. My resistance to him melted more each time I met his eyes. Bull wouldn't have to ply me with gifts or dazzle me with money. His piercing gaze and a simple, 'come here', from him would send me running in his direction. Yes, I definitely need to be in a room where he isn't.

"You're feeling okay, aren't you?"

We walked with his one arm behind my back, his hand cupping my elbow.

"Yes. I'm good. I could make it to bed on my own. The doctor gave me his okay, remember?" I reminded him. "You could go home. I'm sure you've left all your chores undone to babysit me. I do appreciate you but I'm beginning to feel very guilty. How will I ever repay you?"

I didn't look into his face. We were too close. I didn't trust my emotions at this distance.

"We'll chalk this up under the friends system instead of bartering. That way you won't owe me a thing, we're even." He pushed the bedroom door open for me and stayed in the hallway.

"Do you have your nursery list ready?"

"I do. The first one, anyway." Now I did turn to scan his face. "I have to do something for you, Jeremiah. I can't go on taking from you like this. I feel terrible."

"You whip this house into shape for me and we'll be more than even. Do the gardens and square away the inside and I'll owe you, you won't owe me. I'll consider it a favor if you do."

He leaned with his back against the wall in the hall putting more distance between us.

"What do you want done inside?" This was something new, something I could get started on tomorrow if he wasn't around.

"The closets need to be emptied. Anything we can donate, we should. The house is over-furnished, crowded to me but I don't know what to get rid of, you will. Things like that. Put it in a shape to go on the market. Know what I mean?"

"Yes, I do."

"Get your list."

He stood straight, ready to leave. I got the list and handed it to him along with a handful of money.

"I'm going to do up the kitchen and head for home. I do have some things to tend to, you won't see me for a few days. The nursery will deliver to you when you call them and say you're ready. I'll have a few words with Zeke first."

"He won't tell Roy where I am, will he?" I was immediately afraid.

"Not after I talk to him. Don't worry. You have my phone number. You have Alvin's and you have Evelyn's. Go to bed. I'll lock up before I leave. I have a remote for the gate. Goodnight, Iris."

"Goodnight."

I waited until he disappeared around the corner at the end of the hall before I went to sit on the edge of the bed. Half an hour later I heard him go out the front door, heard his truck start in the garage and then the door raise and lower. I went into Mr.

Sommers closet and began folding his clothing.

I had slept most of the day. I was neither tired nor sleepy. By midnight, I had both closets emptied except for my clothing. I found a handgun in the mister's closet. It was loaded. Not a bad thing to have around, I thought. I'd ask Alvin how to work it tomorrow when he came with the recording. If I have a gun, I won't feel completely helpless.

Could you shoot Roy? I asked myself that question. After a moment, I decided if it was him or me, yes, I could shoot at him. I wouldn't like to kill him though—just stop him from hurting or killing me. I examined the gun closely and believed I'd found the safety. I clicked it on and off several times figuring out which was which. I put it in the drawer of the nightstand when I climbed into bed at one am. The little bit of activity, clearing the closets made me tired and I fell into a deep, restful sleep.

I slept until seven, got up and made coffee. As I wandered through the house, I took note of the furnishings and made decisions on what should go and what could stay. The cupboards would be more difficult to empty. How long would I be here using their contents? Should I buy the house? I did like it. I liked the outside areas and the overly tall fences made me feel safe. The thought of living two miles down the road from Bull made me consider the proposition carefully.

Roy had dazzled me with wealth and power. He created unfamiliar feelings in me that I believed to be love because he said they were love. The feelings weren't love. They were caution spurred by self-preservation, adrenalin rushes that my subconscious ignited warning me to flee. That was a tough, painful and dangerous lesson learning those feelings that I should have learned long ago from parents.

Now, Bull raises feelings in me. Strong, sensations that make me warm, make me tingle and are more than pleasant. The problem is that I could be hurt worse than the beatings Roy gave me. Bull has the potential to hurt me badly without touching me.

Bull can hurt me on the inside where the hurt won't show—in my heart and my mind.

I didn't want to forget that the feelings Roy fostered in me were not scary in the beginning either. Don't jump into the emotional pit again, I cautioned myself. You don't know what you're doing when it comes to feelings. You're an emotional ignoramus.

On the plus side of staying, Evelyn is here. She is a friend already. I haven't had a lot of friends maybe none other than Alice, who owned the shop where I worked in Houston. I couldn't count Janet, my attorney, though she had saved me but that was her job, after all, separating me from Roy. There was no one to save me from Bull. That would be up to me.

I'll try it for the time it takes me to get the house and gardens put together. Staying in Littsburg will only be possible if I can develop an immunity to Bull, an aversion to him would be even better. He irks me from time to time but I'm quickly over my temper and adoring him once again. No, I don't think I'll be able to stay here.

That train of thought helped me as I went about the house mentally eliminating furnishings. My decisions were much more ruthless when I was not personally involved. When I would be leaving the house along with the excess furnishings. After breakfast I showered and dressed in my most raggedy work clothes. I carried the bags of clothing through the kitchen into the garage.

Alvin came at eight. He buzzed the button at the gate. I could see him in the monitor mounted above the alarm panel beside the front door. He was backed by a group of teen-aged boys. They must be Bull's crew who were emptying and refilling the planters. The images came from the camera mounted on the house just below the eave on the inside of the fence where no one could reach to tamper with it.

"Good morning, Iris. Feeling better?" Alvin stepped

inside.

The boys grabbed the shovels and wheelbarrows sitting in the courtyard and resumed their work. I closed the door behind Alvin and disabled the alarm so the boys could move freely in and out of the gate with their barrows of dirt.

"Yes, thank you. Come through to the kitchen. Would you like coffee?" I led the way to the back of the house.

"I never turn down coffee. Where's Bull?" He pulled out a chair at the table and plopped down.

"He had work to do at his place. He said he'd be gone for several days." I poured coffee

"That's strange. He has a foreman who's been there forever. He takes care of the ranch, not Bull. I hope to hell he ain't off on one of his crusades." Alvin set a briefcase on the table, pulled out a recorder/player and closed the case.

I rummaged in the cupboard and set a package of cookies on the table beside his cup of coffee. They weren't homemade like Evelyn's cookies. I sat down beside him.

"Ready?"

"Yes." A wave of sickening fright flushed through me. Apprehension at the prospect of hearing Roy's voice after all this time, I imagine.

Alvin pushed the play button and what must be Zeke's voice said,"hello".

"Is this the Smith Excavation Company?" Roy's voice came from the machine, chilling me.

I held my breath. The specter of him looming above me, his features florid in anger made me tremble.

Alvin saw the affect of Roy's voice on me and reached to pat my hand.

"Fraid not. This is the Barnes Nursery." That was Zeke.

"Nursery?" That was Roy again.

"Yes, the plant nursery in Barnes." Zeke was clearly disappointed.

I remembered he was expecting this call to bring him the reward of twenty-five thousand dollars. No wonder he sounds down.

"Barnes, Texas?" Roy was verifying the location.

"That's right, Barnes, Texas. You've got the wrong number, buddy."

"Sorry, I was wanting to hire a backhoe." There was a click. One or both had hung up.

"Well?" asked Alvin.

I swallowed. "Yes," I whispered, "that's him, that was Roy's voice." I shivered.

"Humph," said Alvin, "wish we could get the fella who shot at you to admit Roy hired him but there's no way he's going to talk. Those fellers are well paid and it's as much for keeping quiet as for the killing part."

He shook his head as if to say their nature was beyond him.

"We'll file this information away until we can use it. I'll have my secretary type an affidavit for you to sign confirming you heard the tape and recognized the voice as that of your ex-husband."

He rose leaving the package of cookies untouched.

"I better move on. I reckon I better go check on Bull if it's not already too late. See if I can talk him out of whatever he's fixin' to do. Damn it anyway!" His curse was not addressed to me but, I suspect, had everything to do with Bull.

I wondered what he could possibly mean about Bull.

Alvin left. I got my wide-brimmed straw hat and went

outside to meet the boys. They were busy refilling the planters edging the yard. They were nearly finished with the front. It looked to be a long, slow process. A dump truck had delivered a load of soil beside the drive. The boys loaded wheelbarrows and rolled them inside the fence. Two would team up to lift the barrows and dump the dirt into the planters. There were ten boys working. I hadn't seen the four working outside to scoop the barrows full of the potting soil mix. They had a system that seemed to be working.

I moved a chair to the side, out of their way, and sat down to visualize how I wanted the large pots arranged before they were filled. When I was sure, I drafted a couple of the workers to reposition them before I went inside.

I went straight to the kitchen and poured a cup of coffee. Bull was on my mind. Alvin's words had piqued my curiosity. There was only one way to find out. I got the phone book and looked up Evelyn's number and dialed her on the wall phone.

"Hello."

"Good morning, Evelyn. It's Iris. Are you free? Could you come over? I need to talk to you."

"Is something wrong?"

"I'm not sure. That's why I need to talk to you."

"I'll be there shortly."

"Thank you."

I sat down at the table. Whatever Bull is doing has something to do with me, I have this feeling it does. And, if it has to do with me and my problem, then it has to do with Roy, because *he is my problem.* Would Bull go after Roy? Surely not, I thought, but the possibility made me anxious and full of fear. Roy was wealthy, influential and ruthless. Bull was a naïve country bumpkin compared to him. Roy would deal with Bull as though he was a pesky fly to swat. What could Bull be planning to do? He said he wouldn't be around for several days. Is he leaving town? Is he going to Houston? Oh my God, he is, I know he is, he'll go there and Roy will kill him.

By the time Evelyn rang the doorbell, I had worked myself into a near-hysteric state. She gaped at me in surprise when I opened the door with wild-eyed panic on my face.

"Good grief, Iris, what has happened?"

"Oh Evelyn," I moaned and tears began running down my cheeks, "it's Bull. He's gone after Roy and Roy will kill him."

Chapter Thirteen

"What makes you think that?"

Evelyn stepped inside, shut the door behind her, turned me and prodded me toward the kitchen. In her free hand she carried a wicker basket covered with a kitchen towel. She guided me to a chair at the table, the overstuffed one Bull moved into the kitchen for me, and pushed on me to sit.

"He left last night after dinner. He said he had things to tend to, that he'd be gone several days. I assumed he was going to his ranch to work, you know, to do chores. Alvin, the sheriff, came this morning. He's the one who said Bull was off on a crusade and he hoped he could stop him. Oh, Evelyn, I just know he's going after Roy. He's going to go to Houston, find Roy and tell him to leave me alone. Roy is vicious, he'll hurt Bull, maybe kill him." I sobbed loudly.

"We have to do something, *I have to do something.* This is my fault. If he gets hurt, I'll die, I'll just die." I grabbed a napkin from the holder in the center of the table to dab at my eyes. The tears had come the moment I saw Evelyn's friendly face.

"Calm down, Iris. Whatever happens is Roy's fault, not yours. Bull is not exactly helpless."

She uncovered the basket and began setting items on the table. She'd brought homemade cookies, jam and a loaf of warm bread. The last thing out of the basket was two quart jars of homemade chicken noodle soup.

"I'll put one of these in the refrigerator. They're still warm. You can have some soup and warm bread for lunch." She left one jar on the table.

"What do you mean Bull is not helpless?" I sniffled. In my mind I was visualizing Bull and Roy side by side. Roy was six inches taller and at least seventy pounds heavier than Bull. That's before I got to their personalities. The two were opposites. Good and evil, that's what they were. Bull was the good guy, of course.

"He was in the service, one of those outfits who do special stuff," she said, as if that made him invincible. "He never mentions it. I heard it elsewhere."

"I don't think you realize how dangerous Roy is, and how big. He's nearly twice as big as Bull," I told her.

I was exaggerating but Roy was Goliath in my mind. His hand swinging at me had seemed as big as a wrecking ball. I cringed as my thoughts went to that night when I'd tried to duck from him and avoid the pain when his fist connected with my jaw. His palm stung when he struck me open-handed across the face snapping my head back. He was smiling, his eyes glittered and he drooled in his drunken state. He didn't look human. That was my last beating from him. I thought I was done re-living that night but fear for Bull brought my own fear back to me. After weeks on the run, I had finally quit having nightmares. Then Roy found me and the bullet that barely missed killing me resurrected the bad dreams.

"I'm sorry for all you've been through, but you're safe now. Bull put the word out. The whole town will be on watch. No stranger will get within a hundred feet of you. We tend to our own here."

Evelyn sat primly in her chair, hands folded on the table in front of her.

"I haven't had a chance to thank you properly for finding those insurance policies and having the wits to know what you'd found. There's some that would have tossed them onto the trash pile. Bull says they are good. He's contacted the companies and I'll have money coming soon." She got teary-eyed. "I can't believe it, my worries are over."

I think she was down to her last penny and owed a nickel.

"You're welcome, I'm so happy for you. What will you do now? Will you keep taking in boarders?"

"Maybe. I haven't thought beyond painting the house and making some repairs, a new roof, I expect. What about you? What are you going to do? How are things going between you and Bull?" Her teary eyes sparkled mischievously now.

"Bull and me? There is no Bull and me. He's like you say, the town's most ineligible bachelor."

"Why do you say there's nothing between you? It certainly doesn't seem that way whenever I've seen the two of you together. It's obvious that you are attracted." She leaned across the table, her eyes searching my face for the truth as she believes it to be. Evelyn is pretty sharp.

"Oh, you're right, I'm attracted to him. To tell you the truth, I have no idea why and I don't know what it is I feel for him. I have no experience in romance, Evelyn. My upbringing was void of affection, sterile, you could say. Bull makes my heart pound, I know that." I sighed as I pictured his face the last time I'd seen it.

"He is not interested, though. Oh, he has kissed me a couple times but then he's colder than an iceberg a second later."

"Really! He kissed you? I'd say things are moving along rapidly." Her brows raised in a surprised expression.

"You're kidding me, right?" I'd say her opinion was the ramblings of an old maid except Evelyn has been married. Perhaps I should give her words credence, she knows Bull, I don't.

"No dear, I'm not kidding. If he has kissed you, then he is committed. The problem is he is fighting it, or you, I should say." She screwed her face into a thoughtful expression.

"That doesn't sound very hopeful, he's fighting me?" That made a lot of sense though. It explained his hot/cold attitude.

"Yes. I don't know why or how but, for some reason, he

has decided to be the lone wolf. His parents had a wonderful marriage so it wasn't his home life. I can only surmise that his years in the military brought him to this decision," she said, exhaling a long sigh.

"I've waited a long time, actually, I'd given up on him ever finding happiness until you got off that bus. I think that's when it hit him." She smiled to herself with her memory.

"What hit him?"

"Love." She smiled bigger. She looked blissful.

"Love?" I nearly screeched.

"Oh yes. It was plain as day that he was affected the moment he saw you." She gazed at me as though I was gift-wrapped.

"I was so happy you were coming to my place where I'd be able to keep an eye on what progressed." She laughed a soft chuckle. "I've never seen so much of Bull as I have since you moved into the house."

"You're the one who set us up, having him take me to the nursery," I reminded her.

"You're welcome." She laughed out loud before she sat straight in her chair and asked, "What are you going to do about it?"

"What do you mean? What can I do? He's gone. He's gone and he's in danger."

Panic filled me anew, but this time, the knowledge that Bull cared for me overcame the panic and I began to consider what I could do. What I had to do. I stared at Evelyn as an epiphany struck me.

"I'm going to Houston. I have to save him from Roy. I know Roy and I'll find a way to stop him," I told her, and began rising from my chair.

"Sit." She ordered.

I sat.

"You need a plan or at the very least, a disguise. Bull will not appreciate you showing up like a piece of bait on a cane pole dangling yourself in front of that Roy man. You could blow his whole operation," she said.

"What should I do? How can I find him? I'll call him. What's his number?" I half-rose to get the phone.

"Sit. You can't call. I don't know the number. When he goes off, he can't be reached. I have his number here but he never takes that phone with him. Let's figure out a disguise for you. If you get within a hundred yards of Roy, Bull will find *you*." She leaned back, her index finger on pursed lips and a far-a-way look in her eyes.

"That would work. You get close to Roy, not close enough that Roy could notice you. Bull *will* notice you and connect with you. He's going to be ten shades of angry with you but you'll have to brush that off and stand your ground. If I were you, though, I wouldn't tell him that you came to save him." She laughed at the idea.

"Should I say I've come to help him?" Evelyn was making a lot of sense. I wanted her advice.

"Sure, you could say that or you could tell him you are worried about him. Now, stand up and let me look at you. How can we hide you? Different clothes and a wig, do you think?"

"I just put Mrs. Sommers' things into bags. They're in the garage. She had wigs, too. Shall I get them?"

"Yes, bring some in to try on. We could make you older, maybe even add a cane. It would do double duty as a weapon. I'll make some fresh coffee." She got up and went to the sink.

I ran to the garage.

When I bagged the clothing, I separated the clothes into seasons and I found the spring/summer bags, carried two of them inside and returned for a bag of wigs and another of shoes. Two hours later, we had my new persona designed and perfected. We'd even stopped for a lunch of bowls of soup with bread and jam.

I stood in front of the mirror in the closet and looked at the person I'd become. Her clothing was a bit large but that only promoted the image we were after. The summer dress with three-quarter sleeves hid the youthfulness of my upper arms. The bosom draped in fullness gathered by a belt buckled loosely at my waist to make my waist appear larger and me less curvaceous. A large, lacy collar drew attention from my neck and the wide-brimmed summery hat further disguised my neck and face. We opted for a grey wig in a chin-length style that covered my jawline. I went back to the kitchen and took the gun from the nightstand with me.

"Are you sure Bull will recognize me?" I sat down at the table. "Look what I found in the mister's closet. I think I should take it with me, don't you?" I laid the revolver on the table.

"Land sakes, no. Bull would skin us both alive if you showed up with a gun. First of all, getting it there would be illegal. You can't have much of a relationship if you're in jail. Do you know how to use that?"

She pulled the gun across the table to examine. She flipped on the safety, ejected the clip and looked the gun and clip over. She handled them like a pro.

"No, I don't but you seem to," I said, admiring her ease and dexterity. There must be much more to Evelyn than I thought. I've barely scratched her surface. She re-assembled the firearm, slid the safety on and laid it on the table.

"My father believed ladies should know how to defend themselves if necessary. He was a very modern man for his time, much more so than my mother. She would not have approved of him having insurance, for one thing. I expect that's why you found the policies in the garage." She missed her father, her sorrow showed in her eyes. She shook off the melancholy thought.

"Now, let's talk about what you are going to do specifically." She reached for a pad and pencil lying on the table.

"I'll take the bus to Houston." I watched her write that down.

"Does Roy still live in the same place? How about his business? That in the same spot?"

"I'm sure. His apartment is in a very exclusive building. He'd never give up that address. The same with his business. Appearances are everything to Roy. Should I go to his apartment? Not to his apartment, I mean to the building?"

I was letting her plan my strategy. Cloak and dagger activity was not in my sphere of knowledge or skills. My interests and training were strictly the world of flora.

"I think you should walk the block his building is on about the time you expect he would be returning from work. Stay on the opposite side of the street. Be as inconspicuous as possible, you know, blend in." She was jotting words down on the pad. I couldn't read upside down.

"Tell me what you mean."

"Hide in your character. You're an elderly woman. Walk slowly, lean on your cane. Don't look at him or his car. Does he drive?" Her pencil poised over the pad waiting for my answer.

"No. He uses a car service. He thinks that impresses his clients."

Roy's words spouting the way to success rang in my mind. He refused to allow me to ride the bus. I walked rather than use his chauffeured car. When I was more familiar with the area, I would walk a few blocks from the apartment and catch the bus to work. In the evening, I reversed the process and got off the bus to walk the last three blocks even though I knew Roy was at his office and wouldn't know. I changed into work clothes when I got there and changed out of them before I left the flower shop. Remembering made me realize the multitude of little steps I'd taken to shield myself from his wrath.

"Okay. He's really making it easy for Bull," she said, shaking her head in amusement.

I had no idea what she meant by that. I was beginning to understand that I didn't know Evelyn at all. I thought of her as a ditch but she is much deeper, she is a well.

"That's all? Where should I stay? In the neighborhood or on the outskirts of town?"

Evelyn frowned as she considered my question.

"I'd say on the outskirts of *his* neighborhood. A medium-priced hotel would be good. Use my name when you register. I'll give you some correspondence with my name to make you credible."

She was lost in thought. I sat quietly, waiting for her to continue with her instructions.

"We don't want to waste time. You get packed. I'll go home and get ready then I'll pick you up and drive you to the bus station on the far side of Barnes, in Wildwood, just in case they're watching Barnes. You can be in Houston before morning. Put that other jar of soup in the freezer. I'll take the bread back home with me."

She rose, put the bread in the basket and pushed the bag of cookies at me.

"You can have these in your bag to munch on the bus. Hurry. I'll be back within the hour. I think there is a three o'clock bus." She scurried away.

I sat in awed befuddlement for several minutes reviewing what had transpired in the past few minutes before I snapped to attention and ran to my bedroom to pack. As I'd tried them on for her approval, I'd laid outfits on the bed. Now, I folded them into a suitcase, one of the Sommers'. Roy might recognize mine if he should see me.

I showered and dressed in a pantsuit, blouse, low heels, the grey wig and a chiffon headscarf I could let droop around my face to conceal me. I added some eye glasses that could perch near the tip of my nose. I put a couple of Mrs. Sommers' magazines into one of her totes along with the cookies. What else would an old lady do on a bus? I heard the door bell. Evelyn was back.

"You," she called to one of Bull's teen-agers, "come carry this luggage to the car. Set it in the back seat." She turned to me and gave me the once over, head to foot.

"Good. Nice choice of outfits. Got your cane?"

I lifted it to show her.

"Let's go." She led the way through the gate to her car. "You lay down in the seat, Iris. I don't want anyone knowing you are leaving town."

I guess the half-dozen teen-agers didn't count but I kept quiet.

"You can sit up now but duck if we meet anyone," she said, when we'd driven out of town.

I kept my head down as we passed through Barnes and sat up for the ride to Wildwood.

Evelyn pulled to the curb, angle parking a few spaces from a two-story hotel on Main Street. The town could have been Littsburg but it was Wildwood.

"Here is some stuff with Evelyn Fillmore on it." She handed me a handful of papers. "I'm giving you my driver's license in case you need ID at the hotel in Houston. Sort of keep your thumb on the picture if you have to show it and don't forget to shake, old people shake."

She was giving me last minute instructions.

"I'll go in and buy your ticket. You stay in the car."

"But, what if you get stopped? You won't have your

driver's license." I tried to hand the plastic card back to her.

"Pshaw, Alvin knows I have one. I'll be right back." She bustled into the hotel and emerged shortly with a ticket in her hand.

"The bus will be here in a couple minutes. Let's get your suitcase on the sidewalk ready to go."

I climbed out of the car, forgot my cane and reached back in for it. Evelyn man-handled my large suitcase out of the back seat. The bus pulled in and stopped. The doors wheezed open and two passengers and the driver stepped out. Evelyn pushed me forward and dragged my suitcase after her.

"Get on, dear," she said, for the sake of the driver. "Make sure she gets off in Houston," she told him, as she gave me a covert wink.

I sat several rows behind the driver and sunk low in the seat trying to appear frail and shrunken. I kept my eyes down and got out a magazine after the bus pulled away from the hotel. I was the only new passenger. Wildwood was over five-hundred miles from Houston. I settled myself deep into my seat for the night-long ride. It would likely be sunrise before we got there.

Bull turned into the drive at the Sommers' place. He checked his watch. It was nearly six pm. He wondered if Iris had done anything yet about her dinner. He should have stopped and picked up something at the deli. The large clay pots in the front courtyard had been moved. This arrangement was much better than the old one. He had not intended to come here for at least four days but here he was, the very next day. The woman was driving him crazy. She worried him to death but he couldn't stay away from her. The gate had been unlocked when he got to it. Had the boys forgotten to tell her they were leaving? Had she neglected to lock the gate and activate the alarm system?

He hurried to the door. It was locked. He used his key instead of ringing. The house was deadly quiet. She was probably sleeping. That was good. He could get something started cooking while she napped. Bull went down the hall and quietly pushed her door open to peer inside. He needn't have been concerned about waking her, she wasn't there.

The bed was littered with clothing. No Iris. Now he charged through the house scanning each room as he pushed the door open. Iris was nowhere to be found. He checked the back yard before he dialed Alvin on the kitchen phone.

"I saw her this morning. She listened to the recording of the phone call and identified the voice as that of her ex-husband. I ain't seen her since. I was looking for you but Tom said you was out riding the range. Sorry I can't help you, Bull."

He saw the note pad on the table. He recognized Evelyn's handwriting and read what she'd written. Next he dialed her on the phone. She explained the plan she and Iris had devised and put into motion. Bull listened to her. His head sank as did his spirits. His stomach roiled with dread, fear and anxiety. He ripped the page off the pad and folded it into his pocket.

That crazy, old lady had sent Iris into the lion's den. Worse yet, Iris was expecting to find him there and was coming to save him. Evelyn had been slipping for a few years but everyone knew and she was harmless so they let her be and watched over her. When she took on a boarder, Bull made it his business to ride herd on the situation. The last thing he'd expected was to be smitten by the boarder.

Now, that selfsame boarder was in a life-threatening situation because of a dotty, old woman who'd read too many spy books. He'd intended to address Roy's threats and harassment via the legal system but Evelyn, without realizing, had activated "Plan B". He said good-bye to her and rushed home to pack a change of clothes. He'd have to drive all night to get to Houston before morning.

Chapter Fourteen

Bull threw clothes into a suitcase, added his shaving kit and let his foreman know he was going out of town. He called Alvin and clued him in as he drove toward the expressway in his trip vehicle, a two-year-old Range Rover. He never took the vintage trucks he drove around Littsburg on road trips. He kept them in perfect running order but, they were old and could be unreliable.

"Alvin, I'm headed to Houston. Iris has gone there to save me from her ex-husband, because for some reason, she thinks I went to see him. Her and Evelyn came up with the hare-brained idea. You can just imagine. I need you to keep an eye on Evelyn while I'm gone. She may decide to go to Houston to be backup for Iris."

"Holy cow, when did this happen?"

"After you left the house this morning, I guess. You might tell Calvin not to sell her a bus ticket and have someone take the distributor cap off her car. Warn Carl to be too busy to take a look at it. That should keep her in town. I hope to hell I get to Houston in time to stop Iris from getting killed. Later." He flipped his cell shut and slipped it into his pocket.

He drove the state highways working his way east and north. In Waco, he stopped long enough to eat breakfast at a truck stop. His insides were rumbling. He'd intended to eat dinner with Iris last night. He filled the gas tank and hit the road with just under two hundred miles to go. In five hours he'd covered some three-hundred miles on the deserted highways. He'd left his place at seven-thirty. After the stop for gas and food, his watch read ten after one in the morning. He was making good time. He needed to get there and find Iris before she did anything stupid and by that, he was thinking dangerous, something like making contact with Roy.

While he ate, he pulled Evelyn's list out of his pocket to study. Fortunately, she'd made note of Roy's office and home addresses. Thanks to her notes, he knew Iris was going to disguise herself as an elderly lady and hang out near Roy's apartment where Bull would find her, according to their plan. He couldn't believe Evelyn was able to convince Iris that this was a good idea. But, he reminded himself, Iris did not know that Evelyn was a loose cannon. There had been no reason to tell her of Evelyn's diminishing mental capacities. No one in Littsburg got overly excited when they discovered Evelyn had placed an ad in Texas Magazine advertising for a boarder. After all, Littsburg was one of those last stop, end of the earth places. No one came there intentionally, or so they had thought. Well, Iris *had* come and Bull's affection and respect for Evelyn and his desire to protect her had put Iris smack dab in the middle of Roy's cross-hairs.

Bull programmed both of Roy's addresses into the vehicle's GPS before he left the truck stop. At four am he parked on the far side of the one-way street across from Roy's apartment building, The Washington Towers. Even in the murky pre-dawn light, the building was elegant. He hit the Mobile Assistance button on his rear view mirror and requested the nearest hotels be marked on his screen. According to the *plan*, Iris was to check into a hotel near the Washington Towers. There were six hotels within a five-block radius. The mobile service provided him with their numbers and he began dialing them one by one.

"Good morning, Hotel Fairmont."

"Has Evelyn Fillmore checked in? We have an urgent delivery for her."

"I'll check." There was a short pause. "No sir. Not yet. Would you like to leave a message?"

"No, thank you. I'll check back later." He dialed the next number.

"Good morning, This is the Hamilton Arms. How may

we help you?"

So it went. Each call came up empty. When she wasn't in any of the six, he expanded his search but still didn't find her. Had she gone farther out to stay? Was she using a different name? He leaned against the back of his seat and closed his eyes. What would she do? The problem was he didn't know her well enough to anticipate her. If she were naïve enough to fall for Evelyn's screwy scheme, why would she deviate from the *plan*? That's it, he decided, she wouldn't. She hadn't checked into a hotel yet. Was she in the neighborhood? Was she somewhere close by on reconnaissance?

His eyes popped open and inch by inch he studied the street in front, behind and to both sides of him. In the passenger outside mirror the reflected building behind and across the street had a peculiar bump. As he watched, the bump moved and a second bump materialized at the building next to that one. Bull started his engine, threw the car into reverse and tromped on the gas pedal. The Rover fishtailed as he veered to the opposite side of the street and stopped beside the anomaly. He hit the button to lower the passenger window.

"Get your ass in the car, Iris," he spoke in a low voice that didn't disguise his anger.

The blob pushed against the granite of the building instead of separating from the grey stone. Bull shoved the car into park, slid out the passenger door and grabbed hold of her before she could run.

"Oh, Bull, it's you. Evelyn said you would find me. I was worried, though."

He grabbed hold of her arm and jerked her quickly to the car. He helped her inside and hurried around to the driver's door.

In his periphery, he'd glimpsed a figure stepping out from behind a column that fronted the next building. Bull threw the car into drive and stomped the gas pedal. They careened away from the curb as the very mirror, in which he'd spotted Iris, shattered and fell out of its frame.

"Is someone shooting at us?"

"Yes. Lay down." He took a left at the next corner and drove a serpentine route out of the neighborhood in case the shooter was not working alone.

When it was obvious they were not being followed, Bull pulled over to park in the lot of an all-night diner.

"Where's your luggage?"

I sat up. I'd been laying across the seat with my head on his leg since he'd the same as tossed me into the car.

"At the bus station in a locker."

"Little old ladies don't use bus station lockers. That was out of character." He stared at me in the light coming through the windows of the eatery modeled after a train car.

"I'm not up on the finer points of being a criminal. I didn't want to check into a hotel until I scouted the neighborhood." It was hard to appear indignant when I knew I looked ridiculous. His tone of voice was offensive and condescending though.

"Let's get your stuff and then find a safe place to hole up while we get some sleep. Did you get any sleep on the bus? Have you had anything to eat?" He punched a button and told the mobile service to feed the bus station address to his GPS.

"I didn't sleep. I ate the bag of cookies Evelyn brought me. I was too worried about you. I was afraid Roy would kill you before I got here."

"What, you were afraid you'd miss seeing Roy kill me?"

"You know what I meant."

The ride to the bus station was done in silence. The only

voice was the GPS giving instructions from time to time.

"Give me the key. They may have a lookout in there." He held out his hand.

"A lookout? Who?" My head was spinning, bullets were flying, what had I gotten into?

"I'm guessing Roy has hired himself some security. The fellow outside his apartment for one. Who knows how long he'd been watching you. Lucky he didn't start shooting right away. That makes me think Roy may want you captured, not killed."

He took the key and went inside. I watched through the windows as he went to the lockers, found mine and got my suitcase and tote bag. He put the bag in the back and got back in the car.

"Look." He pointed at a fellow who strolled through the door on the far side and was openly staring at everyone. Even I could see he was searching for someone. Bull had parked on the outer row of the lot and backed in to face the terminal. One end of the building contained the offices and ticket counter. The other, the restrooms and lockers. The ends were brick walls but the space between was floor to ceiling glass on both sides.

"Shall we have a talk with him?" Bull had a devious grin.

"How?" My voice was a croak. Things were moving too fast for me.

"You get out and go inside. Sneak along behind this row of cars and approach the door from that direction," he said, pointing toward the locker end of the station.

"Here's the key, open the locker and put your small bag inside. Look around as though you were trying to be casual and then come out through the same door. Walk back to that end of the parking lot. Got it?"

"What if he comes after me?" I sounded skeptic and I was.

"If he's Roy's man, he will come after you. I'll be waiting

for him. You just walk away like you're doing your old lady act. Let's go."

We got out and he retrieved the tote from the back.

"Don't look for me, that'll warn him."

"Right."

I crouched and skittered to the end of the row, across the end of the lot and stood to approach the door. I used the cane, imagined I was decrepit and moved slowly to the glass doors. I ignored all the people inside and went straight to the lockers. After I put the tote inside, I looked furtively around as though I was guilty of something. Guilty and scared are similar so I did that well. Bull should be pleased. I noticed the man turned quickly away when I glanced in his direction. Good, he noticed me. I shuffled to the doors and back outside where I headed toward the boarding area which was deserted at this hour.

The light scuffle and soft thud alerted me that something was going on behind me. I didn't know if it was okay to turn my head to see what. I went a few steps farther and thought I'd better take a peek in case the bad guy had taken Bull down instead of Bull capturing him. Maybe I should be running for my life.

I wheeled around, forgetting my old lady role. Bull hoisted the unconscious man over his shoulder and cut across the parking lot to his vehicle. He popped the back gate, and flopped the fellow into the cargo area. I ran over to stand beside him. He was opening a satchel and pulled out twist ties and duct tape.

"Get in the car, Iris." He ordered me without so much as a look to see if I was okay. I got into the car.

He was there for several minutes and I heard noises that I imagined were the fellow being rolled around and restrained. My heart was pumping like I was running a marathon. Bull closed the back and climbed in beside me. He dialed his cell.

"Can you meet me at your office? I have a package. Twenty minutes." He hung up and punched an address into the

GPS.

"You did good," he said, as he pulled onto the highway.

"Did you kill him?" I had to ask.

"Don't be silly. If I had, I wouldn't have tied him up." He flipped the turning signal, checked his mirrors and accelerated up an on ramp.

He was right. That was a silly question. He didn't have to talk down to me though. My feelings weren't hurt, I was peeved. I sulked the rest of the ride. He didn't notice. After a ten-minute drive we exited and wove through a warehouse district. The area was rough and rundown. Bull pulled into an alleyway where neither the scarce street lamps nor early dawn light penetrated.

"You stay," he said quietly, as he slipped out the driver's door after hitting the button to open the cargo door.

I heard muffled sounds and realized his prisoner was trying to speak. Bull must have put duct tape over the fellow's mouth. I watched as Bull disappeared through a door that had appeared from nowhere in the corrugated metal of the building. A man met him at the door and he, Bull and the prisoner disappeared. So did the door.

I shivered, hit the button to close the hatch door and reached across the driver's seat to hit the door lock. I slunk down in my seat so my head didn't show above the seat. It was as close as I could come to being invisible. My outside mirror had been shot so I turned the rear view so I could see out the back of the car. I held my breath until I had to gasp air. My heart pounded. I'm not much of a criminal, I don't have the nerves for it.

Bull re-appeared without the prisoner. He yanked on the door then scowled when he realized I had it locked. I reached across to unlock the doors.

"Scared?" He climbed in and started the car.

"You betcha," I said. I was literally shaking.

"Let's go have something to eat before we go to bed."

Chapter Fifteen

I did not want to consider what he meant by that. Would we sleep? Where would we sleep? Separate beds? Separate rooms? I exhaled to calm myself. I'd worry about that when the bedroom door opened. If I thought about it though, I didn't want to sleep alone. I didn't want a room of my own either. My nerves told me we should share a pillow. My hormones seconded the idea.

We drove for half an hour or more, I wasn't wearing a watch and hadn't noticed the dash clock. We turned off the highway at an I Hop. Bull parked in back among the employee cars.

"Take off the wig, the hose, the belt and that god-awful collar. It makes you look like a transvestite preacher. Do you have other clothes or shoes in your suitcase?" He was slinging insults freely.

"I brought some shorts and a tee shirt for lounging around."

"Crawl into the back and change. Hurry, I'm starved."

I climbed over the console and the back seats and opened my suitcase. I found the shorts, the tee and flip flops, undressed and put them on. The old lady clothes went into the bag. As I climbed back over the seats, I met Bull's gaze in the rear view mirror.

"I would have opened the back for you," he said, amused at my climbing around like an errant child.

"Now you tell me." I landed in the front seat beside him and slipped my feet into the flip flops. We hiked around the place to the front door. His arm circled me, his hand rested at the top of my hip in a possessive manner that I didn't mind at all.

When the hostess led us toward one of the tables in the center of two rows of booths, Bull said, "We'll take that back booth."

He walked over and indicated I should sit facing the back of the place and he took the side facing the front door. The hostess followed, gave us giant menus and filled our coffee cups from a carafe she left on the table.

"Can you see the back door?" Bull asked in a quiet voice that wouldn't carry after she left us. For it being so early, the place was half full.

"I can."

"Give my leg a little kick if someone comes through it."

"Like this?" I said and slipped off a flip flop to run my foot from his ankle to his knee over the fabric of his jeans. I raised my brows at the same time.

"You can save that move for later." His gaze burned me.

My little flirt had been turned and used against me. He lifted his coffee and tried it.

"Um m." He made the sound without taking his eyes off of my face and I knew his "Um m." wasn't about the coffee.

I blushed the color of a ripe tomato.

"I like that you still blush at your age. It shows you aren't some used cynic who's seen and done it all." His tone was quiet and sincere. A compliment, I think.

"I have no idea what a used cynic would be. I'm ignorant more than anything, I guess. When I got out on my own, work and school took every waking moment. I didn't have time to dabble in life, know what I mean?" I gazed into his eyes which had yet to move from looking into my face.

"Innocent, not ignorant. Some knowledge only corrupts. You've worked hard and you have succeeded. You can be proud of yourself." Now he did take his eyes off of me to read the menu.

"What are you having?"

"I'd like some pancakes and bacon, please."

"What kind?"

"Buttermilk."

The waitress came. He ordered for both of us. He was having sausage and eggs with hash browns. She went away taking the huge menus with her and the space between us was empty. I decided to "take the Bull by the horns" and talk him out of seeing Roy.

"Why did you come here?" It seemed like a good place to start.

"Why did I come here?" He seem genuinely surprised that I would ask such a question.

"Yes. Why?"

"When do you think I came here?"

He was ignoring my question. I think he cares for me and doesn't want to admit it.

"You came yesterday morning I suppose, unless you drove here after you left me the other night. Did you?"

"No, Iris, I didn't. I did drive all night *last* night after I found out you had dressed up for a masquerade party, gotten on a bus and come here to commit suicide under the guise of saving me."

My mouth fell open.

"What?"

"You heard me. What in the hell did you think you were doing?" He leaned across the table at me and though he whispered, he was plainly angry.

"You didn't come here to see Roy, to tell him to leave me alone?" I was bewildered. How did I get things so wrong?

"Hell, no. I came here because you had to be rescued. I couldn't believe you let that batty, old woman talk you into such a hare-brained scheme. How in hell did you plan to save me? Were you going to wrestle Roy? How has that worked for you in the past?" His eyes were about to pop out of his head. The veins on his neck protruded.

I sat dumbfounded. Unable to speak, my mouth hung open in disbelief. Finally, I squeaked out, "Batty?"

"Yes, Iris, batty. Evelyn has senile dementia. Between us, her neighbors and other townspeople, we watch her closely. She isn't a danger to herself so we leave her on her own in her home where she's happy. Everything was fine until you came along." He shook his head side to side and glared at me.

"I didn't know. She seems fine to me. I came because of the ad. No one told me," I said. Anger and tears fought to dominate me. I was crushed at what he'd said. The truth flashed through my head. He hadn't come to see Roy. He must not care. Evelyn was demented. I'd been an idiot. I couldn't decide whether to cry or scream so I just sat there staring at him, continuing to be an idiot.

His shoulders heaved as he sighed.

"You're right, you had no way of knowing. She managed to put the ad in the magazine without any of us catching on. When I saw her at the bus, meeting you, that was the first inkling we had of what she'd done."

He refilled his cup from the carafe and chuckled softly. He raised his eyes to my face, his eyes were lit with laughter.

"We underestimated her."

I wasn't recovered enough to laugh with him but I could appreciate the prim, elderly woman I'd come to know putting one over on Bull, who'd assumed he was managing her. The more I thought of bossy Bull being hood-winked by an old woman the funnier it became and I did laugh.

"Don't laugh at me," he warned, "she talked you into dressing up in old clothes and riding the bus to Houston." He laughed out loud.

I did, too. In light of my new knowledge, what I had done was utterly ridiculous. Where was my head? I had no idea I was so gullible. I should have known, I'd married Roy, hadn't I? His image made the humor of the situation evaporate. Bull saw the change come over my face.

"What?"

"We poked the bear, Roy, I mean. He'll come after me with both fists now." I trembled at the notion.

The waitress delivered our food. "Anything else?"

"May I have honey instead of syrup?"

"Sure. Be right back," she told me.

"I say, as long as we're here and we've already poked the bear, let's kick his hairy ass," said Bull, as he dug into his breakfast.

How we would go about that, I had no idea but Bull seemed very confident and I had confidence in him. I let go of my fear and attacked my stack of hot cakes. They were delicious. After two of them and my order of bacon, I was feeling good.

"You know Alvin contributed to this farce too."

"How's that?" He had pushed away the platter in front of him having eaten about half of his food. No wonder he looks scrawny, he hardly eats. He hadn't had any trouble handling the man at the bus station, though.

"He said he was going to go stop you from doing something, from going on one of your crusades is what he called it," I told him. "That made me think you were going after Roy and that's why I called Evelyn, I was worried."

Bull smiled and shook his head side to side, bemused by my words.

"Women!"

"Then what did Alvin mean?" I was insisting I had grounds for jumping to the conclusion.

"I suppose he's right. I have been known to go bear hunting before," he said, and laughed.

I knew he was recalling a specific occasion. He got lost in the past, remembering, and sat silent.

I reverted to the past, too. Evelyn had said that Bull was in love with me, that she had seen he was affected when he saw me get off the bus. Now I knew *why* he'd been affected by the sight of me. Evelyn had put one over on him and he was in shock, not struck by love. Thank heavens, I figured that out before I made a further fool of myself by telling him that I love him, too. Good grief, I *do* love him. What a predicament!

"You okay? You look strange." Bull was reaching for his wallet.

I guess we are leaving.

"Yes, I'm good. Thanks for the breakfast."

"Sure."

He headed for the cash register. I trailed behind. He paid and opened the door for me to go out ahead of him. His cell rang.

"Yeah? Thanks." He took hold of my arm when I started toward the back of the restaurant.

"This way," he said, "we're changing cars, mine is going to the shop for a new mirror."

I didn't argue. I went where he steered me. A shiny black Mercedes was parked at the end of the row of cars in front. He reached under the front fender and came out with a set of keys. He unlocked the passenger door with the key fob.

"Get in."

I did. The leather was cool on my bare legs. It felt good. The day was already muggy and it was seven am, typical Houston weather, I recalled.

He drove straight to the Hilton and pulled in beneath the marquee. He popped the trunk before he got out and the bellhop rushed out to get my suitcase from the trunk. I was surprised when he pulled out two bags. By now, Bull had me so befuddled I didn't bother to wonder how my bag had moved from the Rover to the Mercedes. He was Merlin, the magician, but I knew there were people I never saw making things happen. The whole scenario was strange and foreign to me but somehow comforting. We aren't alone. That was the comforting part.

Bull tipped the bellhop and took the bags from him at the desk.

"We'll go it alone," he told the fellow. We rode the elevator to the second floor. I followed Bull down the hall. He stopped at the end of the hall at the stairwell and opened the door.

"After you."

I stepped in and waited for him to lead the way. He went down to the first floor. We came out at the end of a long hall that dead ended into another. I could see the lobby at the opposite end of our hall. I felt as though I was going blindfolded through a maze.

"Never stay above the ground floor," said Bull, answering the question on my confused face. He used the card key on the last door and stood aside for me to enter.

The room was dark and cool. When he shut the door behind us, it was pitch black. He switched on the light in the bathroom which was just inside the door. He walked into the room and opened a door in the wall opposite the bed, flipped a switch and light burst through the doorway. He'd rented connecting rooms. One opened on the stairwell hall and the other onto the hall it intersected.

"Have two exits minimum," he said, continuing my

education into things criminal.

I began to think ahead and hope we were not going to kill anyone, not even Roy. Had we broken any laws? That's when, I realized, we'd kidnapped that man. I didn't even know what had happened to him. Having people shooting guns at you tends to loosen one's morals I decided.

"Where do you want to sleep?" He interrupted my thoughts.

"Wherever you do," I said, and meant it. I wasn't sure I could close my eyes, my nerves were taut. I certainly didn't want to be where I couldn't reach out and grab hold of him.

He must have read my mind.

"Okay, let's shower and hit the sack. You can use this bathroom and I'll take the other one."

I got my toiletries and nightgown and went in to shower. He was in bed when I came out. He appeared to be sleeping. I turned off the lamp he'd left on for me and slid onto the cool sheets.

His voice came deadpan out of the darkness.

"If you want sex, knock on my pillow."

Chapter Sixteen

"I thought people only had sex if they were in love."

Before I turned out the light, I had seen that he was facing the wall, turned away from my side of the bed. I scooted next to him and put my arm beneath his to circle him and rest my hand on his chest.

"I'm not knocking, I'm snuggling," I whispered.

"Snuggling is extra. I'm not up for snuggling. It leads to other stuff that requires knocking."

His bullfrog voice was talking to me, not his "pay-attention, these-are-the-finer-points-of-criminal-activity" voice that he'd used to explain the subterfuge as we'd gone from the lobby to our rooms.

"I came to Houston in good faith to save you. The least you can do is offer comfort when I've been scared out of mind. Besides, you have no feelings for me and sex is for saying you love someone."

I ignored his no snuggling edict and told myself not to stroke his hairy chest with my hand.

"That's where you're wrong. Sex is the four R's. You've heard of the three R's, right?"

"Yes."

"Sex is the four R's, rest, relaxation, relief and recreation. There is no mention of feelings. Whole industries have been built on sex, you got your prostitutes, and their pimps or madams, not to mention how sex has changed history. Nations and alliances were built on sex," he expounded in a dry tone.

I imagined his expression as being wry if I could have seen his face.

"You've missed your calling, you should be on stage doing a stand-up routine." I tapped his rib cage lightly with my fingers. He was all muscle. I couldn't feel bones.

He snorted.

I stilled my hand before it could begin rubbing him and that gave me an idea. I withdrew my hand and bent my upper body back so I could circle his neck with my hands. Then, instead of wringing his neck for being a smart aleck, I began massaging his neck and shoulders.

"This won't be recreation but it should do the other three R's, rest, relaxation and relief," I told him.

"You're laughing, aren't you?" He jerked when my hands circled his neck but he quickly relaxed as I began working the tight muscles.

"Maybe, a little." I smiled in the dark.

As he gradually relaxed, I could feel the tightness leave his muscles and in a very few minutes he was snoring lightly. I wiggled back into position against his back with one arm around him, kissed him lightly on the shoulder and closed my eyes.

Noise in the hall wakened me. Bull lay on his back. I had one leg hooked over him, lying between his legs, my head was on his chest and my arm around him. His arm was wrapped around my back holding me to him. Low voices and bumping luggage meant other guests were checking in for the night. I wondered what time it was but I didn't want to risk waking him by raising my head enough to see the clock on the nightstand.

"It's four in the afternoon."

How did he know I was awake? How did he know what I was thinking?

"Umm," I answered.

"Are you hungry?"

"Yes."

"Do you have anything to wear? I mean something that is not shorts and not old lady. You have to get some clothes today."

He pulled his arm from beneath me and swiveled to sit on the edge of the bed.

"Aren't we going home?"

"We're here, Roy is here, I say let's settle this thing, get it over with so you don't have to look over your shoulder all the time."

He rose and disappeared into the bathroom. I heard the shower.

What is he planning to do? It sounds like he's going to go see Roy after all. Cold dread enveloped me. The warm cozy feeling I'd wakened with was gone. Roy would kill us both. He had men he hired, who would kill us while he watched. I expect he'll want to do me in himself for the satisfaction it will give him.

There's no way Bull can take on Roy and his hired goons. I doubt he can best Roy if they were to fight one another. I would be no help. I can kick, scratch and bite but one fist to my jaw and I'd be on the floor, probably out cold.

"You're not up? Get a move on. I'm hungry."

He had come out of the bathroom wearing boxer shorts with a towel around his neck. His legs which seemed non-existent or toothpicks in his baggy jeans were actually bulging muscles as were his arms. Spray him with oil, tell him to flex and he could be Mr. Universe. The loose shirts and droopy britches he wore disguised a well-toned muscular physique. His black hair was wet and curly on the top where he hadn't all but shaved it as he had the sides. I bet that's why he only takes his hat off to sleep.

I hurried into the other room, showered and pawed through the clothing in my suitcase. There was a long A-line skirt that belonged to Mrs. Sommers. I'd brought a pair of shorty pajamas with a top that could pass for a summer blouse. The skirt was cream and the top was white scattered with pink flowers. My flip flops wouldn't do but there was a pair of beige low-heeled pumps of Mrs. Sommers that would work. My hair was brushed back and held there with some of the bobby pins I'd used to coil it under the hat and wig I'd worn to Houston.

He was on the phone when I came back into the room.

"Right. Call me." He hung up and studied me from head to foot.

"That'll do but let's put shopping first on the to-do list. Ready?"

He was dressed in evening clothes with a white dinner jacket. Where had those clothes come from?

"Yes." I followed him out the door.

"This way ," he said, guiding me to the exit at the end of the hall. We stepped out beside a small garden that separated the hotel from the parking garage. Overhead walkways connected the two on the upper levels. The smell of jasmine permeated the evening breeze. I gasped as my lungs filled with air so humid it seemed liquid rather than gas.

A cab came down the street, Bull waved it down and he spoke to the driver, "Central Mall. Stop at Sophi's."

The drive was short. Sophi's was an upscale boutique. The kind I'd never patronize but the sort where Roy insisted I go to shop. Bull went inside with me after telling the cabbie to wait.

When the saleslady approached and asked if she could help us, he issued a string of commands at her and the next two hours were a whirlwind. She measured me and began bringing outfits for his approval. He would utter a terse yes or no and the article would go on the counter to be rung up or back to the rack. Finally, he took a cocktail dress from her and handed it to me.

"Go put this on."

I did. She brought heels in my size to go with the dress and a designer evening bag. When I emerged from the dressing room, Bull took in the sight of me. His eyes widened slightly.

"Put your hair up." That's what he said to me. Not, that's nice, wow or you look terrific—put your hair up.

I gathered, twisted and pinned it into place.

"She needs earrings," he told the lady, who smiled, nodded and rushed away.

Roy made me have my ears pierced so I could wear glamorous jewelry. The woman brought some gold dangling earrings that accented the gold of my sheath. I put them on. The three-inch open toe heels were also gold. So impractical I thought when I saw them but Bull had given them a thumbs up.

Bull hailed our cabbie, who pulled up to the curb, and gave the driver the name of a restaurant I recognized. The place was in the neighborhood where I'd lived with Roy and was one that he frequented. I started to tell Bull but he had hold of my hand and squeezed it tightly. He was signaling me to be quiet, I think. I shut my mouth without saying a word.

We had been transformed from country hicks to a cosmopolitan couple out on the town for the evening. We could have been on our way to the opera or out for a night of clubbing. The doorman rushed to open the cab door when we pulled up in front of Maurice's. He helped me as Bull got out the other side. I heard him speak to the cabbie.

"Drop the bags at the hotel, change cars and stay close." He stepped around behind the cab and took me by my arm. The cab pulled away into traffic.

The Maitre D's eyes showed shock when he obviously recognized me but not Bull. I had dined here many times when Roy and I were married. He was discreet and didn't address me.

"Table for two?" he asked Bull.

"In a bit. We'll have a drink in the bar first." His arm went around my waist and squeezed me against him as we passed the fellow and proceeded to the posh bar that filled a side room.

Low lights made it difficult to see the other patrons.

I saw Mrs. McKnight first. Roy's back was to me. His mother said something to him and he turned. Our eyes met and his face contorted instantly. Bull was aware and squeezed me tighter.

"Be tough, baby. Be tough. We have him right where we want him." He whispered in my ear as he guided me to a small table and indicated I should have a seat. My fanny had barely touched the chair when Roy arrived.

"What the hell do you think you are doing? That's my wife you've got your filthy hands on." He reached out intending to grab Bull by the shirt front. Bull intercepted Roy's hand with one of his and in one smooth move bent Roy's arm around and up his back. The look on Roy's face now was one of surprise, shock and pain. Bull applied some upward pressure and Roy grimaced and held his breath.

"That relationship wrecked, remember? Isabelle didn't care to be man-handled by a brutish coward. Is that your mama with you? Do you provide security for her? You know, little old ladies get knocked down and robbed all the time. It pays to be careful. I know I intend to be very careful that no harm comes to my girl."

Bull looked down at me, gave me a caress on my cheek with his free hand and glanced toward the table where Mrs. McKnight waited for Roy to return. She was situated so she could not see the straits Roy was in, thanks to Bull. From her viewpoint, they were having a pleasant conversation.

Roy's eyes bulged at the suggestion that his mother could be in danger.

I heard and hoped Bull was not seriously threatening her.

"Tell me you'll be a good boy, tell Isabelle you enjoyed seeing her again, wish us a pleasant evening and I'll give you back your arm," said Bull, with his mouth close to Roy's ear.

Roy hesitated. Groveling was not something he did—ever.

"Unbroken, if you make it snappy," Bull added, applying a tad more pressure.

"Nice to see you," Roy nodded at me. "Have a pleasant evening."

He turned his eyes to Bull asking silently to be released.

"Are you going to be a good boy?" Bull persisted in baiting him.

Roy shook his head in a yes motion.

"Beg pardon?" Bull turned his ear to Roy's mouth.

"I promise to be a good boy," panted Roy, who was in considerable pain by now.

"You bet your ass you will be or I'll kick it up the back of your neck," said Bull, releasing Roy's arm.

Roy immediately began rubbing the twisted limb. His face went from white with pain to purple with rage.

"You just f**ked with the wrong city boy, you little turd." Roy whirled around to stalk toward their table. He veered at the last moment and went into the restaurant entry with his cell phone at his ear.

"Oh my, are you all right?" I peered up at Bull, who was standing beside my chair.

"I am. I believe Roy is calling for reinforcements. Let's have a drink while we wait. Do you want to speak to Mrs. McKnight?" He waited ready to pull out my chair if I said yes.

"Thank you, no. We were never that close. She liked the way I had with flowers but that was pretty much all she liked about me." I rolled my eyes in forbearance.

"You weren't good enough for that pompous shit head she has for a son?"

"Not by a long shot." I glanced in her direction and saw the disapproval on her face. I laughed.

"You are incorrigible. What if Roy comes back with help?"

"Oh, I believe we can count on that. At least, I hope he does, that's the plan anyway."

"I don't have the big picture, do I?"

Bull was definitely up to something and he hadn't shared his ideas with me beyond his thought to settle things with Roy for once and for all. He had bested Roy in the one on one match-up but what about round two? How tough was Bull? Already, he had surprised and astounded me, Roy, too. I was beginning to understand that I didn't know Bull well at all. Was this 'one of his crusades' as Alvin had put it?

Evidently Roy decided to take his mother to dine elsewhere. The Maitre D came and escorted her away. We had drinks and went to a cozy table by the window in the dining room. Bull ordered grilled sole for both of us. Dinner was delicious. I ate like a farmhand in spite of the threat waiting for us outside on the street.

After we finished, Bull said, "Let's dance."

He pulled out my chair and led me to the small dance floor at the back of the room. A five-man combo was playing ballroom music. He put an arm around me and pulled me close. My forehead rested on his cheek and my nose beneath his chin breathing in the faint spicy smell of him.

"I've decided to give in to you," he murmured into my ear.

"You have? About what?" I shivered, though I had no idea what he meant.

"On the sex thing. You don't have to knock. We'll meet in the middle." He pressed me to him.

"We will?" I caught my breath.

"What about the love part?"

"I think you'll be more than satisfied," he whispered, "with everything."

Chapter Seventeen

His nearness or his words made me heady. I held onto him tighter for balance.

"Are you all right, Iris?" He must have felt me wobble.

"I don't know," I muttered. So many strong emotions were coming at me in rapid succession, more quickly than I could process them. Fear, love, panic and passion bombarded me and I wavered on my feet unable to sort which I was feeling at the moment. Fear of Bull being hurt or worse, killed, overcame the others and worry overwhelmed me, worry and fear for him.

"Let's go back to the hotel," I urged him. Maybe we could be gone before Roy's goons arrived. If I could get Bull away, he'd be safe. I'd have sex with him, if he wanted, to keep him occupied and away from Roy. Whatever it took to protect him.

Don't think you are being noble or sacrificing yourself, my conscience piped up. You know you want to be with him. The thought of him and me together filled me and suddenly it was too hot in the room to catch my breath. I gasped for air.

"What in the hell is wrong with you?" He sounded perturbed. "Don't go daffy on me now. I'm going to have my hands full shortly." He gave me a gentle shake.

"Square away, Iris." He was the Commandant speaking to his troops—me.

He shook me out of my little daydream. I was conscious of my surroundings and the impending danger once again. I did a one-eighty and went from a passionate dream to a bloody battle as I searched for ways I could help him or defend him. I'm not strong but until being on the run robbed me of my work, I'd been in good physical condition, not so much these days. Still, I thought, I could pull off one of these spike heels I"m wearing and do some damage swinging the spike at a bad guy's face or groin. The image of nailing Roy with a spike to his groin made me hope that he returned with his men. Of course he will, I told myself. Roy wants to beat on Bull so badly he won't be able to stay away. He'll be here.

The music ended. So did my strategy session. We each had one arm around the other as we turned to walk to our table. A huge brute of a man blocked our way.

"Let's step outside, folks," he said. "We got a little party planned. You're the guests of honor." He chuckled low in his throat.

I felt a poke and looked down to see he had a gun at my ribs.

"If you don't want me to take that from you," said Bull, nodding at the gun, "you'll put it in your pocket. The lady will have a seat at our table while I step outside with you."

"You're not calling the shots, asshole," the man sneered at Bull, "I'm the one with the gun."

So quickly I couldn't see him do it, Bull moved in front of me, twisted the fellow's arm and removed the gun from his hand.

"I guess I am calling the shots after all. If these folks weren't having dinner, I'd jerk your pants down and shove this up your ass." He had the man's arm in the same position he'd held Roy's. "Now, let's escort the lady to her table. Then we'll step outside so I can do just that. Be nice and I'll leave the safety on. Act up again and you'll find gun shot residue the next time you wipe yourself."

He pushed the fellow ahead of us to our table using the man's arm to persuade him.

"Pull out the lady's chair for her and tell her goodnight. Iris, why don't you order coffee when the waiter comes. I'll have a brandy with mine."

The man pulled out my chair with his free hand. I sat

rather than irritate Bull.

"Goodnight," the man told me.

I didn't respond. I watched their backs until they disappeared.

The Maitre D watched them pass and picked up the phone. Was someone calling for a reservation or was the fellow one of Roy's men?

I waited two minutes and followed the men out the front door.

"We'll be back in a few minutes," I told the Maitre D. "We have some urgent business outside." I noticed a flashlight on the lectern that served as his desk and grabbed it.

His jaw dropped but he didn't speak. I hurried out the door, past the valet and turned toward the alley on the far side of the restaurant. The eatery and it's bar took half the block from corner to alley. I didn't think they would have gone around the corner when the alley was the logical spot for an ambush.

The muffled grunts and groans told me I'd come to the right place. The street light on the corner did not reach into the alleyway nor did the small LED lights that outlined the canopy at the entrance to the supper club. The inside lighting was subdued,which made a welcoming impression on arrivals but cast no light beyond the windows.

I stuck my head around the corner to peer into the alley. The space was pitch black. How could they fight without seeing each other? How many guys were in there? Should I turn on the flashlight?

"Bull, do you want some light?" I yelled into the abyss.

"What the hell are you doing out here? Get your ass inside." That was definitely Bull talking.

"What about the light?" I ignored his order.

"Fine! Turn on your light."

I did. Three men lay on the paved passageway. One was on all fours, pants down and I could not believe it, a gun protruding from his back side. He was the man who'd come inside, I think. I immediately shifted my gaze from him. Two more were prone, face down and immobile. Roy was on his knees in front of Bull whose hair was mussed but he appeared unscathed otherwise. I focused the beam on Roy and approached.

"Watch where you step, there's crap all over the place," said Bull.

I went to stand beside him.

"I don't think he's ever going to leave me alone," I told Bull, ignoring Roy as I did.

"Well, we'll see. You stay, Roy." He let go of Roy and went to each downed man in turn and put on flex cuffs he'd pulled from somewhere.

"We don't want to be interrupted, do we, Roy?"

I followed his movements with the flashlight, so he could see to cuff the men. He went back to Roy and yanked him to his feet.

"Iris, go inside. Order our coffee, dessert, if you want some, and my brandy. I'm going to have a heart to heart with Roy. I'll tear his freaking heart out if I have to but he and I are going to come to an agreement. It'll be better if you aren't privy to our conversation. I have a feeling Roy here is going to get bashful. Drop your britches, Roy. Get out of here, Iris."

He slammed Roy against the brick wall of the bar.

"Want the light?" I asked in a voice hoarse with shock.

"That might make things more interesting, sure," he said. "You can hold the light, Roy. It's probably a good idea to have some. I only want to geld you, not turn you into a full-fledged eunuch." Bull laughed a deep, chesty laugh.

I handed the torch to him, turned and nearly ran out of the

darkness.

The Maitre D gave me a searching glance, checking for his flashlight, I expect.

"Send our waiter over, please," I said, in passing. I offered no word on his light.

"Yes, Maam."

I ordered two coffees and two sniffers of brandy. I've never had brandy but I needed something to combat my nerves which were jangling like cymbals. I was visibly shaking and couldn't lift my coffee cup when the waiter served me.

It wasn't five minutes until Bull walked in and took his chair across from me.

"That Roy ain't worth a damn," he said, shaking his head. "He caved before I got the knife open to castrate him. Why did you get involved with such a wimp?"

He brushed imaginary dirt off of his sleeve and reached for his sniffer of brandy.

I gulped.

"You weren't going to do that, were you? Really?" I whispered. My throat had gone dry and my tongue felt covered with sand.

"Sure, I would have. I know what he did to you. I've had it with him, Iris." He was so earnest and matter-of-fact.

"If he comes after you or sends someone again, I'll kill the son of a bitch, I'll kill him dead." He sipped his coffee.

"Mmm, that's good. Arabian, don't you think?"

I reeled in my chair, the room was going dark. Bull jumped up and grabbed hold of me. He held my brandy to my lips.

"Take a sip, Iris." His hand cupped the back of my head.

I breathed in the fumes rising from the brandy and opened

my lips. Bull poured a sip into my mouth. When it hit my throat, I choked and sputtered. My head cleared immediately.

"Okay?"

I nodded. I couldn't speak. My eyes were open and his were only a couple of inches from mine. He lowered his lips to mine and further resuscitated me. The kiss had the opposite effect of the brandy. My eyes closed in warm delight.

He lifted his head and moved back to his chair.

"Sorry, I shouldn't have spoken so indelicately in front of a lady. Sometimes I get carried away with enthusiasm for the job." He swirled his brandy and swallowed a mouthful.

"Roy is a ruthless, unfeeling, narcissistic slug. He'll have to die in order for you to be free of him."

I felt myself spinning again.

"Drink some brandy, Iris and stay with me here." He gazed intently at me.

I took a sip, sputtered and tried to concentrate on his face. Several curls of black hair hung on his forehead. It was a good look for him—a softer look.

"Good girl. What we've done here is set him up." Bull leaned back in his chair and smirked.

"Set him up? I thought it was over," I whispered. I couldn't believe him.

"Oh no, Roy would rather die than lose. That's his Achilles heel. Now, we go home and wait for him. He won't keep us waiting long, believe me. He's impatient, stupid and arrogant, that's a lethal combination.

Are you sure you won't have dessert?" He raised his coffee cup.

I declined with a shake of my head. We finished our coffee and brandy.

"Ready?" He raised his brows to ask.

I nodded again. I was feeling rather done in, like the world after the storm had passed. So much had hit me hard and fast that I was numb, and bewildered. Bull pulled out my chair, I stood mechanically. He realized my condition and braced me with his arm.

"Come on, baby. Let's get you to bed."

As we passed through the entry, I made note of the flashlight on the desk. Bull has great attention to detail, I thought when I saw it.

A shiny black car, but not the Mercedes we'd driven, was waiting in front of the door. The valet opened the door for me, I got in and slid over for Bull to climb in after me.

"We're calling it a day. Take us to the hotel," he told the driver.

We climbed out at the garden outside the exit close to our rooms. Bull did something that worked to make the 'exit only' door open to give us entry. He opened a door into one room, motioned me to wait in the hall and went inside to check before allowing me into the room.

We separated into our bathrooms to shower and get ready for bed. My closet was filled with new clothes from one end to the other. The old luggage from the Sommers' house was gone. Three new suitcases stood on the floor beneath the clothes rod. During our visit to the boutique, I'd been very flustered. I could see now that I must have been comatose. Bull had bought an entire new wardrobe. Items I hadn't even seen were piled on closet shelves or hanging from the rod. There were shoes of every description. Where had they come from?

I showered and slipped into a sateen nightie. Bull was sitting on the end of his bed watching the evening news on television.

"What in the world did you tell that woman?"

"What woman?" He was playing innocent or dumb. I didn't know which.

"The boutique, you know who I mean," I said.

He stood, moved to me and wrapped his arms around me.

"I turned down the bed. Get in." He brushed over my mouth with his lips and walked me backward to the side of the bed. He bent, swooped up my legs, laid me on the sheet, covered me and turned off the bedside lamp.

I heard him moving in the dark around to the other side.

"Damn!"

"What?"

"My toe."

I felt him get in on the far side and prepared to scoot his way to snuggle. He was over me before I could sit up to move. He slid me toward him and lowered his body on top of me.

His hand brushed my hair aside, his lips came down and he kissed me out of my mind. I floated to sex heaven or some like utopia. He took me from delight to delight in an unending sensuality.

When he stopped, I was levitated in an out-of-body experience where I hung suspended in a cocoon of soft, warm rapture. I drifted from there to sleep in his arms.

Chapter Eighteen

Is there anything that man can't do? I asked myself that question as I drifted toward consciousness the next morning. My head lay on his chest again. I moved slowly to a pillow so I could see his face in the light I'd left on in the bathroom when I'd been there after he fell asleep. My face, when I'd looked in the mirror, was pink from his whiskery chin rubbing over me as he made love to me. Did he make love to me? Or, did he have sex with me?

Black whiskers had sprouted longer through the night covering the bottom half of his face. His small short nose was almost blunt on the end, as though it had turned up and been chopped off because he didn't like it. He could probably do that, I thought. His eye lashes were black and lay curled on his cheek beneath the large sockets that held his ice blue eyes.

My fingers had worked through his hair during our long, passionate tryst. His hair was thick, black as coal and even short, it curled tightly. I bet he hates that. It's adorable and I love his hair but Bull finds it a curse, I'll bet.

"What are you doing?"

I'd thought him to be asleep, he wasn't.

"Admiring you," I answered.

"Go shower. I want to get on the road early." He rolled over and sat up on the edge of the bed.

Just like that, the honeymoon was over. Well, I had the answer to my question. He didn't make love to me, he'd had sex with me. I threw back the covers and rushed out of the room before I started crying. I stood under the warm spray of the shower and had a long talk with myself.

You've done it again, Iris, I thought, you've fallen ass over ears for the wrong man. Not really again, I corrected, I'd never been in love with Roy; I'd been overwhelmed by Roy and mistaken awe for love. Why can't I be around a pair of pants without going nuts? Why are my emotions so wrong time after time?

Last night Bull had proved to me that he was a cold, hard customer. He had handled those men like so many carcasses, stacked or hung in a butcher's shop. He'd shown no more feeling than the butcher would either.

Then, he'd dispatched me to Wonderland with his lips and other things that made him every bit as efficient and skilled at lovemaking as he was at fighting. He must think me a loose, easy female with no morals. Who could blame him? Not me. I am the idiot with no morals.

I started to dress in a pretty summer skirt and a white sleeveless blouse but changed my mind and put on walking shorts, a tee tucked in and some skimmer tennis shoes. Who knew what today would bring and I should be ready to run for my life. I folded the rod of clothing into the new luggage. It took all three suitcases to hold the things he'd bought. I made a mental note to go to the bank and get money to pay him when I got to Littsburg.

He wasn't in the room when I came out. Someone tapped on the door. I peeked through the lens to see the bellhop and opened the door.

"Morning Maam, your husband is waiting out front in the car. He sent me for your luggage."

I grabbed the handbag I'd set out and followed the cart down the hall to the lobby and out to the car. We were back in the Land Rover. I noticed the broken mirror on my side had been replaced. I reached for money to tip the bellhop.

"The mister took care of me," he said, and shut my car door. He waved as we pulled from beneath the awning into morning traffic.

"I want to get out of the city before we stop for breakfast," said Bull, who had yet to look me in the eye after spending a good portion of the night using me for his satisfaction. He did the four R's at least four times.

Don't be sour grapes, I chided myself mentally, you were more than satisfied, remember? I did remember but I didn't want warm, wonderful thoughts about Bull. I was his passing fancy and I shouldn't get hung up on him. I wouldn't. I'd cross him off—been there, done that! That's how I'd handle him.

I was lost in inner conflict and not listening.

"Iris!"

I jumped when he all but shouted at me. "What?"

"I said there's a cup of coffee to hold you over until we stop to eat. Is something wrong?"

I couldn't believe he said that and he'd said it without even glancing my way.

"Why would anything be wrong?" I muttered and reached for the coffee in the console cup holder. I sipped the coffee then sat back with my eyes closed and faked sleep to make not speaking to him easier. The ruse worked very well and I actually fell asleep. We'd had a short night, sleep-wise.

"Iris, wake up. Iris!"

Bull's voice woke me.

"What?" I mumbled.

"We're going in to eat. Are you hungry?"

"Yes." I glanced at him.

He was staring at me.

I turned away, got out of the car and headed for the diner's door without waiting for him.

He caught up with me. "What the hell is wrong with you?"

I stopped and breathed fire at him as I let go of my pent anger.

"Wrong with me? Nothing is wrong with me. I'm always a bit testy after I've been . . .been . .you know what I mean."

I stalked away but he grabbed me by the arm and swung me around to face him.

"So that's it. I figured we'd get to that. I had brandy. I lost my head. You didn't seem to object so I supposed it was okay to continue. I thought you enjoyed our time together." His jaw clenched and I swear his eyes were blue ice.

"Oh, I did. You did swell, thank you for screwing me around." I pulled my arm free and went inside.

The hostess showed us to a booth of Bull's choosing which meant the back most one. I ordered for myself before he could ask what I wanted. He ordered, handed the waitress his menu and glared at me.

"You're being very childish, Iris."

"I had brandy, too." I wish I'd held onto my menu so I'd have something to hide behind.

"I take it you haven't had sex with very many men," he went on. Fortunately, no other diners were seated near us and he kept his voice soft and low.

"Since I notched my belt this morning to account for you, I have two. I'm thinking I'll quit there. I don't think the third man is the charm, do you?" I put all my hurt and anger into my words.

"I hurt you, didn't I?" He had blinked when I laid into him and he had an expression on his face as though he'd kicked a puppy by mistake.

I didn't want or need his sympathy.

"Don't be silly. You taught me a lesson. I'm fine. Here comes our food."

The waitress saved me from further examination by him. I forced a pancake down my throat which was constricted nearly closed with emotion. Life had inured me to situations like this. It was only that I felt so much for him that the hurt was magnified a hundred times over.

"Don't worry," I said, after I'd poked down several bites, "I'll get over it. No harm, no foul, right?" I stared across into his eyes.

His expression hardened for a brief moment then his gaze softened.

"I'm sorry, if that helps."

"Immensely, thank you so much. Excuse me." I slid out of the booth and hurried into the ladies room. I held a wet paper towel to my face and counted slowly until I had my emotions under control.

He was gone when I returned to the booth.

"Your husband said to tell you he'd be at the car. He needed to make a phone call." She smiled as she gathered the dishes from our table.

I'd eaten one hotcake and Bull had barely touched his sausage and eggs.

"Thank you." I walked slowly outside. I hadn't noticed the time and didn't know how long I'd slept. I hoped we were close to home.

"Ready?" He asked when I got to the car.

"Look, this is awkward. Why don't you find a bus station and drop me off. I'll ride the bus home." I gazed across the hood of the car, the fight had gone out of me. I wanted to curl up and mourn.

"Get your ass in the car, Iris." He climbed in and pushed the button unlocking my door.

I got in.

"Do not swear at me again."

"Stop being a baby."

"You hurt me!" There it was out.

"No, you're fine, remember." He clamped his jaw tight and started the car as he swore under his breath, something like blankly blank brandy.

My thoughts, as we careened down the freeway, were he must be in a hurry to be rid of me, and my other thought was of our night of passion. I let myself relive the moments dwelling on each word, each caress, each nuance. Bull was thoughtful, gentle and he was loving. He was not a man out to get sexual relief, he was making love to me. I hadn't been mistaken, after all. Brandy be dammed, I decided, he was lying through his teeth.

I turned in my seat enough to gaze at him without getting a crick in my neck. After enduring several minutes of my scrutiny, he spoke.

"What are you doing, Iris?" He stared at the road. He should be able to feel my eyes on him, I was certainly staring hard enough.

"Trying to figure out what you're up to," I said, calmly and without the rancor I'd used earlier.

"What have you come up with?" He glanced at me.

"Well, to put *my* thoughts in words *you* will understand, you're a lying son of a bitch. But, I'm not finished analyzing you yet. Ask me again, later."

I quashed the smile on my face and stared down the road, same as him. My thoughts returned to our night of passion and I sighed very loudly. A quick, sideways glance told me he'd picked up on the sigh *and* its meaning. He very nearly smiled.

"You think you're pretty clever, don't you?"

Was that sarcasm I was hearing from him?

"Yes, I believe I am. Kudos to you, though. You almost

had me believing you don't care." I shifted to get the better view of him again.

"That wasn't nice at all, doing me that way."

"I'm not known for being nice."

"What are you known for?" I hoped if he answered I wouldn't be sorry I'd asked.

"That's above your pay grade," he said, and he chuckled.

I ignored his remark. "I know something you are good at if you want to give my name to the ladies as a reference.

"Thanks but I don't need references."

"Really? You're that well-known in romantic circles? I'm surprised I haven't heard about you but then I've been sheltered." I poked at him because I could see his discomfort.

"That's enough, Iris."

"Yeah, sure, honey." I reached over to rub my palm up and down his leg.

He glared at me.

I patted his leg and turned in my seat to face the road

"I think I'll take a nap."

He didn't reply. I closed my eyes.

The smell of food wakened me. I sat upright and blinked, looking around me. Bull stood at a drive-up window outside a fast food place. I spotted the door marked restroom on the side of the building and hurried over to go inside. I used the facility and washed my hands and face before I joined him at the window.

"I ordered you a burger and fries with a shake," he said.

"Thanks, that sounds good." I stood close and reached over to rub my hand up and down his back. That got me a stern glare.

"Is your back sore, honey?" I was rubbing him the wrong

way—on purpose.

"Enjoy yourself while you can." He smirked at me, pulled some cash out of his pocket and handed me the shakes to carry. I followed him to a picnic table in the shade. There was a nice breeze.

I unwrapped my burger and bit into it, juice ran down the corners of my mouth. He laughed and reached across to mop my chin. When I was able to swallow, I complimented him on his choice of eateries.

"Did you know about this place or is this a happy coincidence?" I sucked a mouthful of cold ice cream through the straw in my shake.

"I have stopped here before."

I tried the fries—hot and greasy. Delicious.

"You need to understand about last night," he said, his manner turning serious.

"I believe I understand perfectly. You made love to me. You're sorry you did. You don't want to be involved with me but you love me." I held up one hand and ticked off on my fingers as I recited each circumstance.

"Nothing can come of last night. You need to understand that."

"Why? Are you married?" That thought occurred to me as it popped out of my mouth. Good grief, what will I do if he says yes.

"No. I'm not married." He held up his hand and began ticking off *his* reasons one by one.

"I'm forty-four, too old for you. I do dangerous jobs from time to time and I cannot risk your being hurt or killed. Some of the people I deal with are very dangerous and by that I mean, killers. And, last of all, I don't have the time or the inclination to take on a relationship." He had four fingers sticking up.

168

"You are not too old," I said, in rebuttal, raising a finger.

"You don't need to do dangerous jobs, you can do other work." My second finger joined the first.

"I saw you take down four killers by yourself last night. I even lent a hand or a light." Finger three.

"You love me, I can tell and neither one of us is getting any younger so quit wasting time." Finger four and my thumb shot up. I waved my hand in his face, stuffed in a mouthful of fries and winked at him.

He rolled his eyes.

"You're not changing my mind, Iris."

"We'll see, honey. We'll see." I winked again.

He rolled his eyes.

Chapter Nineteen

"You don't know what you're saying. You just got out of a bad marriage. Why would you get into a bad relationship? You don't know what you're doing. The proof of that is, you married Roy. You need to get your head on straight." He put the last bite of burger into his mouth and tipped up his Styrofoam container of milkshake to wash it down.

"Eat up. I'd like to be home before dark." He wiped his chin with a napkin and began gathering the trash from his meal.

"I know what I'm doing," I said, "I did learn a lot from Roy, all of the wrong stuff, I know wrong when I see it and I know right. You are right for me. You need very little fixing." I added my wrappers to the bag of trash he was holding.

"I am not right for you," he argued, "you're being foolish." His eyes were flinty as he glared into my face. He was perturbed, that was plain to see.

"What needs *fixing* on me?"

Ah, so he did hear that part.

"Oh, I think once you quit ordering me around by telling me to get my ass here or there, our problems will be over."

"Get your . . .get in the car, Iris." He blushed, I think.

"Right, honey." I hopped up and hurried over to the car.

He took the bag of trash to the barrel and sauntered to the car.

"How much farther?" I asked when he got in.

"Couple hours. You can take a nap."

I wasn't sleepy, I'd been napping but I agreed.

"I believe I will. You kept me up most of the night." I

think he blushed—again.

I lay across the seat and put my head on his thigh, closed my eyes and sighed.

"Dammit, Iris! Stop it! Sit up and behave yourself." He stomped the accelerator in a fit of temper or exasperation.

I was in the act of sitting up and nearly flew off of the seat when he realized he was the one being foolish and raised his foot. I crashed against the dashboard and slid to the floor.

"Son of a bitch."

I jostled a second time as the car screeched to a stop and rolled off the road. I felt a final jolt as he shoved the gear to park. He reached down to pull me onto the seat.

"I'm sorry. Are you all right? Tell me you're all right?" He turned me to see my face.

I blinked to clear the confusion after being thrown around unexpectedly. My hand automatically went to my head, my most recent injury. His hand covered mine and brushed back my hair.

"Did I make you bump your head?" His face was knit in concern. His hands slid to my shoulders and he crushed me to his chest and let his arms circle me.

"I'm sorry, I was acting like a shit head. Please say you're okay." His mouth moved to my ear to whisper to me.

I squirmed until I could put my arms around his chest.

"I'm pretty sure I'm fine. I should have had my seatbelt fastened. Sorry," I said, to make him feel better.

He held me away from him to look into my face again. For an eternity he stared into my eyes and I stared back.

My heart burst as I saw the feelings he couldn't hide.

"I love you," I whispered.

His face twisted into anguish.

"I'm no good for you."

"You're perfect." I leaned in and kissed him softly on his lips and settled into my seat.

"I'll fasten my belt." I did as I said.

He pulled back onto the road, slowly and carefully. We drove for an hour without speaking a word. I didn't look in his direction. I figured he was busy recovering or re-arranging his life to accommodate me. I hoped it was the latter. I couldn't rush him, I knew that. Bull is a stubborn, set-in-his-ways man. I'll have to bring him around a bit at a time if I can bring him around at all. Lordy, I hope I can, I'm crazy over him.

"I wonder if the boys are finished with the planters."

"I expect so. You'll have to call the nursery. I told him not to bring anything until he heard from you." He gave me a quick non-committal glance that told me he had himself back in control.

"Thank you. I'm going to need help when I order my trees, you know, to re-pot them. Could you give me the numbers for some of the boys? The strongest ones?" I laughed.

"Trees?"

"Yes, I'm planting small, decorative trees in pots to give the yard some shady areas. Wait and see. I think you'll like it."

He met my gaze for a brief moment before he shifted his attention back to the road.

"So, you're planning to hang around Littsburg?"

The question came softly, hopefully or is that wishful thinking on my part?

"Absolutely. I have long-range plans." These plans had popped into my head this very minute but he didn't need to know that.

"What plans?"

"Maybe I'll buy the nursery in Littsburg and have a combination nursery and vegetable farm. My private farmer's market. It's just an idea. I'm thinking about it. I haven't seen the place yet." I leaned back against my seat, closed my eyes and imagined Bull and me standing in front of baskets of produce, surrounded by three, tiny children. I smiled, it was such a happy thought.

"Stop it, Iris."

I opened my eyes. "Stop what?"

"I know what you're doing. I can tell by the look on your face. You're planning everything out, happily ever after. You, me and probably a child."

"Three, I'm thinking."

"You're only making things worse, harder on yourself. I don't want to hurt you but it ain't gonna happen. I don't know how else I can say it so you'll believe me." He shook his head unable to comprehend me.

"Don't worry about me, I told you, I'm fine." I studied the scenery. "Why didn't you warn me about Evelyn? I may not have gone running to Houston had I known she has dementia. I would have tried to reach you first by phone."

"Actually, Houston turned out well after all. Roy is going to come busting down here as quick as he gets the crap from that alley scrubbed off and some clean clothes. He may have trouble finding guys to come with him after what happened to the last bunch, but he'll have help, I know. We'll have him in our yard this time." He chuckled softly at the thought.

I didn't find it amusing. I shivered.

"I didn't tell you about Evelyn because I didn't think you would hang around once you got a good look at Littsburg. You appeared to be a big city girl the day you got off the bus. I figured you'd be gone on the next one." He shook his head as though he couldn't believe I was still here.

"I love a small town. I'm all about people, plants and dirt. I could even do without the people." That was true. If I had Bull and my plants, I'd be in heaven. A man to love and my plants to keep me busy.

"You're a regular Pollyanna, aren't you?" He gazed at me for a moment with what I interpreted as a tender look.

"I expect you're right, I am. When you grow up without a family, you cave or you take happiness when you find it and you hang onto it." I shook off the solemn thought. "That explains why I get along so well with plants. Plants aren't nearly as demanding as people."

I stared out the side window, hiding my emotion from him. He went silent and we rode a long time without a word.

"Do you need anything from the store? This is the last town of any size until we get home."

I roused from my daydream of planting the pots and planters and thought about bread and milk.

"I should get a couple of things. Will I be able to go out when I get home? To the store, the bank?"

I wondered what the new routine would be. Could I be a normal person for a few days before Roy came to town breathing fire to exact revenge on me and Bull? Bull is number one on Roy's list of people-I-want-to-kill, by now, replacing me. I doubt if killing Bull only once will be enough for Roy. An image of his face, florid with anger, rose in my mind. He would be livid after Bull bested him and his men in that alley. When he rolled into Littsburg, he'd have his gun loaded for bear.

"Tell you what, tomorrow I'll take you to the nursery, both if you want. After that, you have to stay in and keep your head down. You can be in the yard working but I want you behind the walls of the fence. Will that do?" He very nearly smiled.

"I'd like that but don't you need to be getting ready? For Roy, I mean. He's going to be a maniac. You beat him *and* those men with him. He would go ballistic if I wore the wrong dress. You don't realize how bad he can be," I said, hoping to convince

Bull to round up an army.

"Bad is something I *do* know about," he said, and he grinned with a mischievous look I'd seen rarely, usually when he was planning to annihilate someone.

"Roy's temper works against him. He doesn't think, he acts. That's bad form." Bull laughed out loud.

He pulled into the lot of a supermarket.

I checked my handbag for cash. He saw me.

"Have enough?"

"Yes, thanks."

I went inside and in spite of only needing bread and milk, I filled a cart. Bull waited in the car. He was leaning on the front fender, busy on his cell when I came out. I told the bag boy to put my things in the back seat and climbed into the car. Bull talked for several minutes more.

"Is everything all right?" I asked, when he got in and started the car.

"Fine," he said, "just fine." He grinned again.

I'm beginning to think he's enjoying himself. Should I be feeling sorry for Roy? No way! Roy deserves whatever Bull can deliver and I'm beginning to realize just how much Bull is capable of and thinking Roy should be running for the hills.

The Sommers' house looked like home to me when Bull pulled into the drive. He raised the garage door and drove in, closing it behind us. It was pitch black with the door down. He used the headlights to find the switch by the door into the kitchen.

I got out and opened the car door to carry groceries but he stopped me.

"Let's check the house then you sit in the kitchen while I bring in your things. You have been in the hospital, don't forget." He went in ahead of me and searched the whole house. He checked the yards, front and back, too.

"Sit," he commanded. I sank into the overstuffed chair he'd put at the table for me.

In very few trips he had the groceries and my suitcases inside. The luggage he carried to the closet in my bedroom. The groceries were set on the kitchen table.

"Want me to unpack these for you?" He nodded at the brown bags filling the table top.

"Thanks, I'll do it so I know where things are. Would you like me to make you some dinner?"

"No. I have to get home. Call if there's a problem and this time, call me—not Evelyn. Got it?" He tried to be stern but wasn't.

"Got it. Thanks for the rescue. Good night." I trailed him to the door and reset the alarm after he left.

After the groceries were stowed and I'd unpacked my new wardrobe, I mixed a huge meatloaf and put it to bake. I could eat cold meatloaf or make sandwiches with it for days. I put together a large salad and stored it in a plastic container ready to dip out by the bowl. I did the same with a mixture of fruit which I coated with pineapple juice to stay fresh. There, my meals were ready for two or three days. I wandered outside and walked around the house taking stock and imagining what I would do, what I would plant where and my problems dissipated as I pictured the finished yards.

My fears of Roy and the frustration of Bull evaporated. I lost myself in the vision of what would be in a few weeks where empty pots sat now.

I heard the buzzer as the oven announced the meatloaf was done. I set it on top of the stove to rest and dialed Evelyn on the kitchen phone.

"Hello, Evelyn, it's Iris. I wanted to tell you I am home safe. We were wrong, Bull had not gone to Houston but he did come and drive me home."

"Oh, that's nice, dear."

"Yes, it was. He saved me a long bus ride. How is everything with you? Do you need anything?" I pictured her standing at the kitchen phone in her house dress and apron.

"No, I have everything. A check came from that company Bull wrote to so I have money in the bank. I'm having a new roof put on the house. I hope they don't step on my flowers."

"Warn them to be careful. I'm happy about the money your father left you. I have to go, Evelyn. Call me if you need anything or come for coffee."

"Bye, dear."

I hung up and wondered how Bull had managed to get the insurance company to pay up so quickly then shook my head. Why do I question anything that man does? I ate dinner, showered and went to bed early. It had been a hectic couple of days and I was anxious to get to work in the morning. I could partially fill the big pots with soil while I waited for Bull to show and drive me to Barnes.

I set the alarm for five but I shut it off and rolled out of bed before it went off. I slipped into my favorite raggedy shorts and shirt, made coffee and took a cup outside to sit on the step and watch the sunrise.

I heard him before I saw him. It was early, just after six. He started when he saw me.

"You're up," he said softly.

"Yes."

He sat down beside me on the step and set a cup of coffee from the Quik Shoppe between us.

"You're out early. Reconnaissance?"

"No. More of a review." He gazed at me with a searing scrutiny that made my stomach flare with heat and my heart do the roller coaster thing.

"Let's go inside."

I rose and led the way into the house. He was right behind me, close enough that it was hard to breathe. When we got to the kitchen, he set my cup and his on the counter, put his arms around me, his lips on mine and I don't remember much after that.

He loved me out of my mind. It was Houston all over again. He worked me and my senses over until I was numb from pleasure before he raised his head to gaze into my eyes.

"We better get dressed and hit the road." He sat up and began putting on his clothes.

I ran to the bathroom for a very quick shower. Bull's patience is shorter than his whiskers. I didn't take time to wonder what had spurred this romantic interlude. When I got to the kitchen, he was looking out the window over the sink drinking his coffee.

"I haven't eaten. Do you want some breakfast?" The clock on the stove showed it was eight-twenty. We had spent two hours in bed. The time had passed in a flash. We had cuddled between bouts of lovemaking, stroking each other, learning the other's body, silently communing.

"I ate. Make it snappy. I have an appointment later." He didn't so much as glance at me.

That explained our morning sex. He was doing the Four R's. I bristled at being 'used' that way as I made toast to eat on the way to Barnes.

"If you're busy, I could get someone else to drive me and have them deliver."

He wheeled around at the sound of anger in my tone. His arms circled me. He kissed me. "I'm sorry. Please hurry."

I buttered my toast, grabbed my purse and headed for the door.

"Let's go."

The urge to question him ate at me but instead, I ate my toast and rode in silence. He had sought me out and wasn't that what I wanted? I believe I know enough of his character that he has feelings for me or he wouldn't be in bed with me. I have to let him set the pace for this romance that he won't admit we have going on. The phrase "enough rope to hang himself" came to mind. I smiled.

"What's funny?"

"You."

Chapter Twenty

His expression said he didn't care for being labeled "funny". He didn't say anything only glared ahead. I chewed my toast and watched the road. I was determined not to rush him or push him by flirting with him, making a move on him or forcing discussions about 'us'. He didn't want to admit there is an 'us' so I'd play blind, too. I could act as though having torrid, unbelievably marvelous sex on a casual basis was something I did everyday every bit as well as Bull could.

When we got to Barnes, I reviewed the list Bull had given them to deliver and added to it as I walked through the nursery. I filled several wagons with plants. Bull loaded the wagon and delivered each load to the front. I made arrangements to have everything delivered today, paid and walked out to the truck.

"I'm really excited. Can you get a couple of your boys to come today. I'm not sure I can lift the larger trees without help. Do you have time?"

"Sure. Only two?"

"Four would be better. Thank you. Can we stop at the Littsburg nursery before you drop me?" I was deliberately hiding any sign of affection for him and being careful not to show interest in him. He could well have been my brother if a person judged by my attitude toward him. I thought he seemed puzzled by my behavior, I wasn't calling him honey or reaching to stroke him. I ignored his curiosity and acted as though I didn't notice.

Mr. 'Bull' Jeremiah Jackson was going to have to make the moves in this romance if any moves were made. Let's see how long he can keep up his indifferent attitude with his hormones running amok. I wondered at the kind of night he must have had that he was at my house to take me to bed at six in the morning. I'll bet he hardly slept and figured he'd get to my place before I was out of bed. He'd planned to crawl right in with me. I just know he was.

I filled the back of his truck at the Littsburg nursery and met Gladys. We could have talked flowers forever but Bull was pacing. I could see him out the corner of my eye. I cut our conversation short and promised to come visit her soon.

"She'll be closed the rest of the day," said Bull, as we drove away toward home.

"Why do you say that?"

"You bought everything she had. What are you going to do with all of this stuff?" He sounded testy.

I expect he lied about having had breakfast.

"You'll see." I had bought two more huge pots from Gladys. They were three feet tall and the mouth a good eighteen inches across. I wanted to plant twin mimosa trees in the pots I'd place just outside the French doors opening out of my bedroom at the back of the house. Gladys had a nice collection of night blooming jasmine. I bought five three-gallon buckets. The scent would filter into the bedroom. I'd add a couple of chairs, one for me, one for Bull. I exhaled a sigh of satisfaction as I pictured the grouping and the two of us enjoying a glass of wine in the twilight.

He shook his head over my sigh. Bull finds my displays of exuberance, happiness and affection to be too much. Worse than those emotions are tears, he cannot deal with tears. I'll do my best but I cannot go forever without crying.

Bull made a phone call from my drive and said the boys would be there within the hour. We unloaded the pots and the buckets of jasmine. I'd have the boys carry them to the back when they got there. The rest of the plants were set beside the drive. The boys could carry them to their places for me later.

"Is that it? You need anything?"

"No, I have everything, thank you. I could make you a

quick sandwich for the road. I have leftover meatloaf I made last night."

"Thanks but I'm in sort of a hurry." He turned away and strode to his truck. I watched him disappear and shut the gate.

I went inside to have a sandwich before my workers arrived. It was noon.

The truck from Barnes came at the same time as my work crew who unloaded the plants in record time. I played traffic cop and stood inside the gate directing them where to place each pot and bucket.

We made huge strides during the long afternoon. I began by teaching them how to plant a tree in one of the large pots and they worked in pairs filling the pots and planting trees until the ones in front were done. While they transplanted the trees, I worked filling the planters that edged the stucco fence. I enlisted a couple of the fellows to help me place and plant the large bougainvilleas in the corners where I could train them to grow up along the top of the fence.

Three ten-foot tall desert willow trees were manhandled into three gigantic pots. It took all four boys and me to get the job done but once we had them planted in the pots we'd situated beforehand, their lacy canopies shaded the wrought iron table and chairs. The effect was striking. The magenta and pink blossoms of the trees made the courtyard come alive.

"Wow," said one of the guys, Mike, I think was his name.

"Yes," I agreed. I gave them a short rundown on the trees as we sat beneath them enjoying some bottled lemonade I'd picked up at the store. By the time we knocked off at six that evening, the planter edging the fence along the drive was filled as was the stretch bordering the street in front. The planter from the street to the back yard was filled halfway to the house. The boys agreed to come again tomorrow by eight in the morning.

If Bull came again tomorrow, I hope he came earlier. I didn't think it was a good idea for the young men to find me entertaining a man so early in the day.

I filled a plate with a slice of cold meatloaf, piled on a heap of salad, carried a bowl of fruit and silverware in my free hand and stuck a bottle of water in my pocket. I went outside to eat under the willow trees. The firecracker Penstemon played against the soft color of the stucco walls. I'd planted them in clusters of seven. The sage green of the Agave complimented their flaming red orange. Purple verbena was planted in three's every few feet down the planter. Tall Ocotillo rose in clumps with vermilion blooms on the ends of each upright spear. I planted a variety of small succulents around the bases of the clumps.

The gray green of the shrub commonly called Texas Ranger echoed the Agave's muted green. The shrub was covered solidly with yellow flowers when there was humidity or rainfall. I planted Mexican poppies, desert marigolds, red yucca and yellow bells, too. Every inch of the planter was filled as far as we'd gotten. There were spaces here and there for effect and accent. The purples, yellows, reds, magenta, and various shades of green had transformed the courtyard into something spectacular. The arrangement of willows with the seating area was magnificent. Ficus, mimosa, bottle brush and cascading plum trees filled a dozen large pots we'd arranged strategically.

It grew dark and I went inside, put the kitchen in order and showered off the grime. I locked all the doors but when I got to the French doors in my bedroom I couldn't resist the sweetness of the night jasmine drifting into the room. I left the doors half open to enjoy the scent. Why not? The fence was eight feet high, thanks to Mrs. Sommers' paranoia. The alarm system was first class The garage and the gate were impenetrable.

I crawled into bed and rolled over to breathe in the faint scent left by Bull this morning. His leathery, brown face with the perfect nose, heavy brows, and black whiskers rose before me in the darkness. He was handsome, very much so. He was everything I wanted in a man. Everything any woman would want.

His attitude could stand some improvement but I think if he ever admits that he loves me, he'll do a complete turn around. Being intimate with Bull is fulfilling and life changing. When I compared Bull and Roy, they were good, and evil in every aspect. Roy was wicked, frightening, and a bully. Bull only bullied bullies. He isn't perfect, he is bossy but I'm beginning to think that is his defense mechanism. He grumbles to cover his feelings. He's very good at grumbling.

He makes no excuses or explanations when he comes calling, like he did this morning, for intimacy. What do they call that? I remember, it's a booty call. I'm a booty call for an irascible grump of a man who I love dearly. I won't tell him that, though. Thoughts of him and his undercover skills put a smile on my face, made me look forward to morning and put me to sleep.

I listened. I didn't know what wakened me but something had. I held my breath and strained to hear. There it was, the distinctive squeak of the door that led into the kitchen from the garage. Bull had called my attention to it the first time he showed me through the house.

"I could fix that for you but that squeak is an early warning system. If anyone tries to get into the house through that door, you'll hear the squeak and you'll know exactly where they are," he said.

Having a warning system was fine with me, I was very jumpy those days. Who are you kidding, you still are, I thought. I slid out of my bed, squatted next to it and arranged my long body pillow beneath the covers to look as though someone was sleeping here. The bathroom and closets were dead ends where I could be trapped. I went to the French doors and peered out around the sheers blowing into the room with the night breeze.

The coast was clear. There was no sign of anyone. Moonlight lit the area outside the doors. I spied the huge pots the boys had moved back there this afternoon and did not hesitate. I threw a leg into a pot, thankful I hadn't added any dirt yet. I stood in the pot and bent to pick up one of the buckets of jasmine sitting beside it. I crouched and sat on the bottom of the pot and held the jasmine steady on my knees which were pulled up against my chest. I ducked my head so it fit beneath the jasmine and hoped I was hidden from sight.

Pffffft, Pffffft, Pffffft, Pffffft. The sounds were close. They came from my bedroom I realized at the same moment I recognized them as gunshots. There had been four shots and the shooter was using a silencer. That smacked of a professional. Bull is rubbing off on me. I froze as I listened to the sound from inside.

"Son of a bitch, she's not there."

"What do you mean she's not there?" That was Roy's voice.

"I mean you just drilled a pillow full of holes. I thought you said she lived here. I don't like this. First there was that guard outside and now she's not here. We're being played. I'm out of here."

"Wait, she's hiding. I know she is. She must have heard us. Let's search the house." That was Roy not wanting to give up.

"You can do whatever the hell you want. I'm leaving. If you have any sense, you'll get your ass out of here, too. This smells like a trap." The quiet rustling of their movement died away.

I think they left but I'm too frightened to look. I settled myself more comfortably down into the pot and tried to breathe without making a sound. I fell asleep.

This time voices wakened me. My work crew had arrived. After I recognized their voices, I raised the jasmine.

"I'm here in the pot. Someone take this plant." I held the jasmine over my head. One of the boys took it from me and two others helped me crawl out of the pot.

"Two men broke in last night. I heard them and got out of bed and hid here. They shot my pillow full of holes. I have to get out of here but nobody can see me leave," I told them.

They could hear that I was on the border of hysteria.

"Do you want to go to Bull's?" One of them asked. "We wondered why we found the front gate open this morning. It looks like someone prised the lock. There's a hole in it, too."

"Yes, Bull's, I want to go there. How can we sneak me out of here and out to his place?" I scanned their faces.

"Easy, get back in the pot. We'll carry the pot to the back of the truck and drive you to Bull's. If you keep your head down, no one will see you."

"That will work."

I slung my legs back over the rim of the pot and curled around the inside of the pot.

"Can you see me?"

"Nope. Let's go. One on each side of the pot." One of the boys had taken charge.

I felt the pot being lifted and carried.

"Set it down. We have to open the gate."

I jarred against the side as the pot lit on the paving. They picked the pot back up and settled it in the back of the pickup one of them was driving.

"Two of you get in and hold onto the pot. We don't want it sliding out."

I heard the engine start and felt every bump in the street. The ride was smoother once we turned onto the highway. I had just one thought. I hope Bull is home. When the pickup veered into the drive I rolled in the pot and then we came to a stop and I jostled again.

"What are you boys doing here?"

That was Bull. I stayed curled in the pot. If I've learned anything lately, it's that you never know who is watching you.

"We brought you this nice, big pot from Iris," piped up one of the boys.

"The hell you say. Why would you do that?"

"She's inside of it," said one boy.

"Someone tried to kill her last night," chimed in another.

"She got away and hid. We brought her here and kept her out of sight. You want us to carry this pot into the garage, Bull?"

He was a minute answering. "Yeah, carry it in, boys."

I felt myself being handled again. Then I heard Bull.

"Hello, Alvin? Get over to the Sommers' place. Someone tried to shoot Iris last night. You better see what happened to Gunther." There was a pause. "She's okay I think. She's here at my place. Call me when you know what happened. Set her down right there, boys."

I looked up to see Bull staring down at me. He shook his head, an I-can't-believe-this shake. He extended his hands and I glommed onto them. He pulled me upright.

"You okay?"

I nodded. Seeing him always takes away my bravado and I collapse in his presence and become a crying heap of mush. He lifted me out of the pot.

"You go through this door. The breezeway will take you into the kitchen. Stay there."

He turned to the teenagers.

"Better not go back to Iris' today. Alvin is going to check out the crime scene." He pulled a wad of cash out of his pocket and counted some into each of the four hands.

"Thanks men. You did good." He turned to walk them

back out to their vehicle. I went into the house.

I was at the sink looking out the window at some big construction project going on back of his house.

"Building another barn?"

"Sort of." He slipped his arms around me, resting his hands on my hips and his chin on my shoulder.

"You sure you are good?" He kissed up and down the side of my neck.

I nodded an affirmative.

"Have you had breakfast?" His hands met on my abdomen and pressed me against him.

"No."

"Want some eggs?"

"No. I'm tired. I've been in a pot all night. I want to shower and lie down."

"First, you eat. He opened a cupboard and set a toaster on the counter. He got English muffins from the fridge, butter and marmalade. When those were on the table, he seated me.

"Eat!"

His cell rang.

"Yes, Alvin. You sure he's going to be all right? Good. Forty-five caliber huh, that's serious fire power. Let me think a bit. I'll get back to you." He sat down across from me.

"We had a man watching your place. He was supposed to call Alvin and me if anyone showed up. Someone shot him in the head. That's why he didn't call us."

"Oh," I sucked in my breath. "Is he dead?"

"No. He has a plate in his head from being in the service. The shooter hit the plate. Gunther lost a lot of blood but he's going to be fine. He slumped over when he was hit and no one could see he was in the car.

Come on."

He guided me from behind into his bedroom and then his bathroom. He fixed the shower for me and left the room. He was back in time to dry me, dress me in one of his shirts and love me out of my mind.

Chapter Twenty-one

We lay in his bed enjoying the closeness being alone and together.

"I want you to know something right up front, Iris, in case you want to get out of this before it goes any farther." We lay on our sides facing each other.

"What are you talking about?"

"You and me."

"You mean us? Is there going to be an us?" Be still my heart. I didn't expect this . . .not this soon anyway.

"It seems like it. Every time I turn around, you're there. I can't seem to break free of you." He talked gruff but his eyes said differently. They were lit with warmth and, I think, love. I chose not to remind him that he had come calling on me, not vice versa.

"I have caused you a lot of trouble."

"That you have. But, that's easy to get over and I don't mind cracking heads. What I want you to know though, is that I'm not going to have a dozen, frilly, little barefoot girls with runny noses under foot. You can back out now and I'll understand."

"I don't believe I ever said a dozen, six maybe."

His expression had changed.

I believe he is scared. Of what? That I'll say it's over? He must think I'm going to be a terrible mother. Runny noses!

"You said three, not six. I'll settle for one. Let's see how that works out before there's a second one. Agreed?"

I guess this marriage is going to be a dictatorship but I get to agree or disagree. What would happen if I disagreed? A bigger thought struck me. Married! Was he asking me to marry him? No, he's articulate, he wouldn't hint around at something like marriage, would he? Maybe, he would, he has a problem with emotions both with having them or witnessing them.

Suddenly I could see him on his back in the middle of little girls who had his dark curly hair and tiny nose. They were climbing on him and he was covered in chubby little arms and legs and laughing. He was going to be a great dad but now was not the time to tell him. I'd let him learn on his own, one baby at a time.

"Sure, we can do it that way, I guess." I sounded wistful —on purpose.

He gazed at me and his face softened, "Okay, two but that's it. We'll see how they do."

"You're not going to make them work or jump through hoops, are you? I mean, babies are babies, Bull, they're helpless."

"You know what I mean, we'll see how well we can handle them and if we can do it right, the parent thing. Then we'll see about the third one."

"Whatever you say." It was easier to agree with him for now. He'd come around as soon as he got his hands on the first one. I hope.

"Did you see the men who broke into the house? What wakened you? How many were there?"

Fun, fuzzy warm time was over. We were down to business again.

"It was the alarm system that woke me and by that, I mean the squeaky garage door. Remember when you told me you wouldn't fix it because it would squeak if someone opened it?" I reached over to cup his jaw with my palm.

He's not much for sweet, tender moments but I tried to drag this one out. He rose up on his elbow and I lost my hold on him.

"What else?"

"I heard them talking and there were only two voices. One of them was Roy. He shot the pillow thinking it was me. He shot four times. I could hear the sound of the gun going off."

"Tell me everything they said."

I repeated their words. They hadn't said much. I think I got them right.

"Then they left," I said, when I'd gone through all I heard.

"And you curled up in your flower pot and went to sleep," he said, and he looked astounded and amused.

"You did just right." He sat up and moved to the side of the bed. "So, Roy came to town. I'm a little surprised by that."

"Why? What do you mean?" I sat up, too.

"Roy is a coward. I'm surprised he beat you up by himself, that he didn't have backup to hold you down. The fact that he came to town to pull the trigger himself, means he's madder than he is afraid. Roy is one of those people who let their emotions run them. They don't stop to think, know what I mean?"

I thought back to my life with Roy and how quickly he could fly into a rage if no one was around and how he stifled his anger temporarily if his mother or associates were present. The look on his face at those times told me I was going to be in for it later. How I'd want to get up and run where he'd never find me. I shuddered.

"Yes, I know exactly."

"Let's get dressed and since I don't have any big pots except the one you came in this morning, let me show you where to hide if the need arises."

"You're not leaving, are you?"

"I have to go to town and see what's going on. I want to know how they sneaked up on us this way. I didn't expect them to come this soon or I'd not have left you alone. I figured Roy would take a couple of weeks to plan his next move but he's obviously too impatient. I underestimated him or mis-estimated him. He's angrier than I thought. You must be one mean mama to upset him this way."

He stood and came around to help me up from the bed. He was on the verge of laughing.

"Let me go with you. I'll stay on the floor of the car." I was not over last night. I didn't want to be alone.

"I'm taking a truck and I can't risk them seeing you. Right now they don't know where you are but they'll find out where I live and figure you're here. We have a short window of time here to get ready. Come into my closet. Let's find you something to put on."

I followed him into a huge walk-in closet. He rummaged on a shelf and handed me the bottoms to a set of long underwear.

"These may be kinda warm for today but if you have to go to the cellar, they'll feel good. Here's a tee shirt."

I carried my outfit to the bedroom and slipped into the stretchy spandex underwear that fit me like leggings. I wonder what they look like on Bull's legs which I know now are quite muscular but trim. I pulled the tee over my head and went into the bathroom looking for something to use on my hair. I found a comb.

Bull came in dressed in his usual droopy pants and faded shirt. He was wearing those awful looking boots.

I looked him up and down and shook my head at him.

"And you wondered why I offered you money," I told him. "You look like a refugee from a rodeo."

He wagged his heavy black brows up and down at me.

"Turns you on, right?"

"Right."

I laughed at him and marveled at how far we'd come that he would and could act the clown with me.

"This is the best my underwear has ever looked," he said, snapping the elastic waist of the drawers I wore. "Come on."

He led me through the house to the kitchen, where he flipped a switch on the pantry wall, and out a door onto the back porch. Across the lawn was a small mound about four feet high and maybe ten feet across. The mound was covered in some kind of blooming vine which I didn't recognize. Bull led me behind the miniature hill. He reach down and pulled open a door. Steps led down. There was a light down there. That explained the switch in the pantry.

"Go down and look."

I stepped carefully into the opening and down the eight steps counting them as I went. Bull followed me down. A cozy nest was at the bottom of the steps. There was a daybed made up with blankets. An easy chair set by a plastic tube that allowed a small circle of sunlight to shine down. Shelves were stocked with canned food and books. There was even a toilet behind a curtain suspended on a rod. I stood silent and amazed.

"It was build for a tornado shelter by my grandfather. I've updated it," he said, nodding at the toilet.

"You see this lever?" He pointed to a bar beside the steps. "You pull it down and the door closes and locks. Lift it and the door unlocks and opens. There's a little camp stove if you want to make coffee or heat a can of soup. I'd rinse any pans before I used them."

He wagged his brows again. Sure enough, there was a small sink.

I turned on the faucet and water came out. I shook my head in disbelief.

"Now, during night hours, you need to cover the skylight

so no light escapes. Turn this wheel and the cover slides over the light. You won't give away your hiding place. If you suspicion anything, act on it, don't wait. Turn on the power to the cave, you saw me do that in the pantry, and get yourself down here fast. Roy and his henchmen can't penetrate these walls. Bullets can't either."

He turned in a circle pointing out white plastic circles in the walls.

"These are windows," he said, about the six-inch circles. He used a knob on the plastic circle to slide the cover up and I peered through vines and saw the back of the house.

"You'd want to turn off the lights at night before you look out. The switch is there by the stairs." The tour was complete. He led me back up into the sunshine.

I gazed around. The garage extended beyond the back of the house and blocked off that side of the yard. The new building going up on the side opposite the garage is big. It's framework reached twenty feet into the air. The roof was odd the way it was portioned into squares. I couldn't imagine it as a finished structure.

My attention was drawn from the odd structure by the arrival of the shaggy, giant dog I'd seen here on my first visit.

"See anything?" Bull was talking to the dog.

The dog laid down.

"That's a no," Bull explained to me. "If he'd seen anything, he would take off in that direction to show me."

"What's his name?"

"Chester. I just call him 'Dog'. He comes to either." We walked to the house and Dog came along.

"I'm headed into town. Do you want anything?"

"No. Well, some clothes would be nice. Is that possible?"

"I'll see. If I pull into the garage and anyone is watching the house, they won't know what I'm up to but I can't promise."

"I understand."

"Now, if Dog comes running to you, get into the cellar. If he just walks up and lays down, there's no problem but if he's antsy, he's warning you. Understand?"

"Yes," I said, gazing into his stern countenance, " mind the dog."

He rolled his eyes and kissed me goodbye.

"I think I like you," he whispered.

I watched until he disappeared behind the trees screening the house from the highway. Dog ambled off into the same screen of brushy shrubs and trees. Is he doing a perimeter check? I sat down in the big rocker on the front porch. The porch was smooth, painted concrete. It was painted dark brown to match the logs of the house. I gazed around at the property. That would be a good place for a hammock, I thought as I sized up the corner of the porch. A hammock would make a nice spot to nap. I studied beyond the porch. A thickly wooded area shielded the house on that side, too. Beyond the woods or in a line with them would be the huge old barn. I should go look in there, I've never gone past the garage. Some other day, I decided, I was very comfortable.

I heard barking then Dog came out of the woods in front of the house like a shot. I didn't hesitate. I was in the front door, tore through the house, flipped the switch in the pantry and out the back door without stopping to think.

I took time to close the kitchen door behind me. No sense advertising which way I'd gone. Dog came careening around on the porch from the front as I flew down the steps and across the lawn to the shelter. I reached where I'd seen Bull reach and my hand closed over a knob. I pulled and the door lifted. Dog and I ran down the steps and I yanked the lever to lock us inside and whoever was out there out.

"Good boy," I whispered to dog and stroked his shaggy head. That's when I noticed the blood on my hand. I squatted beside him and found they had shot him in the leg. It looked as though the bullet had grazed his leg, not passed through or gone in deep. Thank goodness. Knowing Bull and his obsession with preparedness, there would be a first aid kit here somewhere. I found one on the shelf and cleaned and bandaged Dog's leg. He didn't squirm but lay quietly while I tended the wound. The bleeding stopped when I applied a bandage.

With him seen to, the next order of business was our intruders. I rose and went to the window opposite the stairs. That was the one where I'd had the view of the back porch. I watched and waited. Several minutes passed and I thought I could detect movement in the kitchen. The overhang of the porch roof shaded the house making seeing inside difficult. Nighttime with lights on inside would be no problem but I couldn't be certain I was seeing someone in there. I kept watching. Dog lay on a rug on the cement floor. He was certainly at ease. Maybe there was nothing to worry about—then I remember the gunshot wound to Dog's leg.

After what seemed like an hour, the back door opened and two men crept out onto the porch. One was Roy, the other fellow, I didn't know. Both had guns in their hands, guns with very long barrels. Silencers! The stranger pointed at the mound concealing me and signaled Roy to go one direction while he indicated he would go the other way. I let go of the window knob and it slid shut. Dog growled low in his throat. I patted his head and shushed him quietly. He went silent. I grabbed a flashlight off of the shelf and turned the handle to close the sky light. I didn't like being blind but I didn't know if they could break the skylight if they found it.

I couldn't call for help. I think my phone may be in the bedroom at the Sommers' house. Bull thinks of everything. Why doesn't he have a phone in his shelter, his panic room. The idea of this being a panic room occurred to me, probably because I was in a panic. I used the torch to find my way to the daybed and called softly to Dog to join me. He came and sat down next to my feet. I put my arm around his shoulders and wished I was in town with Bull. I hope he doesn't spend hours there checking things out when what he's looking for is in his own backyard.

The concrete walls of the bunker plus the insulation provided by two feet of soil piled over it deadened any sound from penetrating its walls. Suddenly I could hear faint thuds, far-a-way pounding. I rose and went to one of the windows. Yes, one of them was beating on the window. I could feel the vibration of the hammering when I put my fingers against the plastic. Would it break? How had they found it? The beating stopped. I was hearing something, maybe far off gunshots? I couldn't tell.

I was terrified. What were they doing out there? I heard a buzz. I listened. There it was again. I looked around me frantically. There, on the shelf, a red light was blinking. I shined the flashlight that direction and saw the red light was coming from a bulb on an old-fashioned phone. I picked up the receiver.

"It took you a long time to answer. Did I catch you at a bad time?"

Chapter Twenty-two

"No, now is good. What's up?" Relief flooded me when Bull's voice asked the inane question. I responded in kind. He laughed in my ear.

"Yeah, I'm pretty sure I like you. Why don't you come out and say hi to Roy? Alvin and a few of the boys are here, too. Is Dog with you?"

"He is. They shot him in the leg. We're coming out." I hung up the phone. "Come on, Dog, we're outta here."

I pulled the lever by the door, heard the lock click open and pushed up on the door. Sunlight nearly blinded me after the short time in the cellar. I shaded my eyes with one hand as I scanned the group of men for Bull. He grabbed hold of me from behind.

My eyes were adjusting and I saw Roy lying face down on the lawn. He was dressed all in black, black sweat pants, black tee, black shoes. Did he think he was a ninja? Bull could give him some lessons on how to do that. His hands were cuffed behind his back.

"Uncuff me, I want my attorney. I'm going to sue your ass for assault. When I get done with you, you'll be sorry you ever laid hands on me, you deputy dawg dumb ass." Roy strained to raise his head to see Alvin as he ranted at him. The veins on his neck stood out.

How many times had I seen him like that? Too many.

Bull stepped forward, placed a scruffy boot on the back of Roy's head and ground his face in the lawn.

"That's enough out of you," he said, as he applied a final thrust of force that made Roy moan in pain.

"Watch out you don't step in that mess," he cautioned, as

he guided me to the porch and into a chair.

Roy's sidekick was a big fellow. He sat with his hands cuffed behind him on the lawn a few feet from where Roy lay with his nose bleeding after the grinding it got from Bull's boot.

"Get me a doctor. Damn you. Everett, you piece of shit, do something." Roy turned on his partner lashing out at him for the bad turn things had taken for them.

"Shut your f**kin' yap," said the big fellow, scowling at Roy, who was rapidly building into a temper tantrum.

I watched as he rolled to his side and ranted obscenities at everyone, his face turning florid as he spat his venomous bile. I saw him for what he is, a twisted, sick bully. He didn't frighten me. He sickened me.

"Can they get him out of here?" I asked Bull, who stood beside my chair.

"Anything you want, honey. Scrape up that piece of crap and take him away, will you, Alvin. Iris is sick of looking at him. Can't say I blame her, he is a sorry excuse for a human being and sure as hell ain't a man, are you, you yellow, woman beating, weasel, wimp."

As he spoke, Bull had gone to Roy, grabbed him by the waist of his pants to lift him to his knees so he could kick him in the backside hard enough to send Roy flying forward to land on his bloody nose.

"I hope I didn't get crap on my boot," he said, looking down at his feet, "I know Iris is fond of this pair." He glanced my way to wink at me. I rolled my eyes at his little act.

That wasn't my final glimpse of Roy though, I'd face him in court about a year later when I testified at his trial. My time and my life from that day to the trial have been the happiest days of my life.

After Alvin and his deputies took Roy and his henchman away, Bull and I sat in his kitchen having lunch.

"I have to go home today. Those plants scattered all over the courtyard need to get into the ground. I need to soak those trees we planted yesterday."

"I suppose you'll want to ride home in that big pot you came in," said Bull.

"Not really but I am taking the pot. It's one of a set. I need it."

"You're going to leave me without a pot?" He looked so ornery. I couldn't believe he was making such a bad joke. I ignored his attempt to be funny.

"Will you come have dinner with me?"

"No, but I'll come sleep with you. I've got a lot to do. I'll be there before you go to bed, though. I got a look at what you've done so far this morning. It doesn't look like the same place. You have a special gift, Iris. I suppose you won't want me to sell the place now."

"I thought we were going to be together."

"We are."

"Where will we live?"

"Where ever you want."

"I don't care where we live as long as we're together. I figured we would live here, in your house." When I said that, he looked relieved.

"I'd like to live here. I'm used to it. Dog wouldn't like to move, not sure he would even if I asked him to. There's lots of room for your little people to play. I'm glad you see it my way," he said, and I could see he was glad, indeed.

"I called the boys this morning and told them to be at the house at two. You'll have to get a move on," he said, glancing at his watch.

So, he'd had a pretty good idea all along that what went down this morning was going to happen. I suspected as much.

"Did you know Roy was here, at the house, when you left this morning to go to town?"

"Well, they didn't hide very well. Dog put me wise to them. You did great, going to the cellar like I told you. You're very reliable. It's great to know I can count on you to follow instructions." He turned serious for a moment. "That's important, Iris, that I can depend on you to do exactly as I say."

I gazed into his eyes. He had accepted me, he was taking me on though I could tell that he'd never meant to have a partner, a wife. What had he been involved with that had made him the loner he is and made him a man who wouldn't risk being close to another person for their sake and for his own emotional well-being?

I looked at the clock on the wall. It was one-thirty.

"Are you driving me?"

"I will do that, are you ready?" He pushed his chair back and stood.

"Yes, let's go load that pot." I walked out the door with him trailing behind me.

"Change your clothes when you get there. You shouldn't be bending over in front of those boys in that underwear. They do great things for your fanny."

I looked back over my shoulder at him. He had an evil grin.

"I think you mean my fanny does great things for men's underwear." We lifted the pot into the truck. He lifted the tailgate so it couldn't fall out if it got jarred in route. I climbed in the passenger side. He was taking the truck with the gearshift on the floor. I glanced from it to his face and back. He had the grace to laugh *and* he had a guilty look on his face.

"You *were* feeling me up," I roared at him. That devious devil. He didn't answer me. He laughed.

"You are not to be trusted," I told him. He laughed

harder. Ah well, who cares, I asked myself. His actions led to our being together and now I know he can laugh.

We spent two more days planting and arranging the outside of the Sommers' house. I put in a kitchen garden of herbs and vegetables in the planter close to the kitchen end of the house. Pots of herbs set close by the kitchen door along with a small table with chairs for outside dining. Each evening when he came to spend the night with me, Bull circled the house admiring the new landscape and making comments. We did sit with glasses of wine beneath the mimosa trees outside of our bedroom.

"Are you finished?" He gazed at the courtyard around us. The soft, violet rays of the setting sun had dropped below the top of the stucco walls and we sat in semi-darkness.

"Yes, outside. I'd do much more if we were going to live here but I won't for strangers. Their tastes could be different from mine. I'll start in the house tomorrow. May I send a few things to your place? There are some furniture items I like a lot. If it's okay with you, I'd like to keep them."

He reached for my hand, an uncharacteristically romantic move for Bull. He put it to his lips and kissed my fingers.

"You may rule the houses and the out-of-doors. The garage is my domain. You may visit me there. You may not plant, rearrange or supplement the area. Your small descendants are not allowed."

"You worry me with your anti-child remarks. I'm afraid you won't love our children." I captured his hand before he could turn loose of mine and kept us connected.

"I'm sure they'll grow up to be pleasant people," he said, "if we do right by them."

"I see. Are you worried about being a good parent?"

"The problem is I've never been attracted to babies and children. It seems they are always crying, screaming or letting their noses run." He shrugged his shoulders saying it was simple, he wasn't into little people.

"My babies are going to be beautiful, and sweet and never ever have noses that run without being tended to."

"Then I'm sure I'll like your children."

"But, they won't be my children, they will be our children," I was beginning to have a terrible feeling that we weren't meant to be together. That was something I wasn't prepared to contemplate.

"If those little people have one little pore of yours, I'll think they're keepers. I'm sure they'll grow on me, you did." He smiled and kissed the back of my hand.

"Let's go in and make one of them right now. That'll show you I'm serious." He pulled me up from my chair, covered my lips with his and backed me into our bedroom. I couldn't tell him I may already be pregnant because he kept his lips on mine.

I emptied the house of the kitchen equipment and boxed it for the Salvation Army store. Bull insisted he either had or would procure (his word) any kitchen gadgets I would ever want so I stripped the Sommers' house bare. Excess furniture was donated to the Salvation Army along with boxes of knickknacks. I chose some chests and small tables to keep that Bull hauled to his house.

Evelyn came for coffee. She had to hear all about the show down with Roy. She asked a million questions. We had cookies she'd baked and brought with our coffee. I set the rest of the bag beside my purse to take home to Bull.

"Did you show me the trees you set outside of the bedroom? Bull mentioned them. I'm going to run back and look real quick." She jumped up, grabbed her purse and took off in that direction.

"Go ahead. I'm going to rinse our cups." I had brought a couple of coffee mugs in from Bull's after I packed off the ones in the cupboard. I wrapped the cups in paper towels and set them next to the cookies and my purse.

"That's very nice, dear. I have to run. I'm stopping at the market on my way home. Say hello to Bull for me. I think it's wonderful that you two are getting along so well. Bye." She came in, said a hurried goodbye and rushed down the hall toward the front door.

Bull came in, they must have met at the front door.

"Did you see Evelyn?"

"I did. She was in a hurry. Are you ready? I want to get to City Hall before they close." He picked up the sack of cookies and helped himself.

I locked the kitchen door and checked the windows. I went around to the other doors while Bull munched the rest of the bag of cookies. We walked out of the front door together and he locked it. I handed him my key.

"There you go, landlord. My work here is done. What do you need at City Hall?" I slipped my arm through his and matched my steps to his.

"Evelyn bakes a mean cookie," he said, popping the last of one into his mouth. "Marriage license. Thought we'd take care of that tomorrow."

"Are you asking me to marry you?" He was so complacent. We could have been talking about where to go for dinner if I went by his attitude.

"No, I'm saying we'll get married tomorrow. I thought it was already settled that we were going to be together. Are we not?" He was staring dumbfounded at me.

"It's just that I cannot recall you ever asking me to marry you. You have never said that you wanted to marry me. I'm not sure if you have feelings for me. I've told you I love you. You've never said you love me. I got married once when I shouldn't have, Bull. I need to know that this time it is right, that this time is forever. I think you don't take this seriously."

"There's no way to be more serious than getting a marriage license. I'm not a heart on my sleeve guy, Iris. You'll have to take me like I am. Now get your ass in the truck," he ordered, holding the door open for me.

"I believe we were dropping references to my fanny as part of our new relationship," I said, looking into his eyes from my perch on the seat of the truck.

"You're right. I'm sorry. Honey, would you pretty please elevate your backside into the vehicle?"

"Sure. Just as soon as you kiss me." I was half in-half out sitting on the edge of the seat with my feet hanging out. He was in the door waiting to close it. He was deliberately being mule-headed and ornery and I was being petty and demanding. We had a little stare down. He stepped close until he was pressing against me.

"Now, what did you want?" His voice was a whisper.

My hands cupped his face. I kissed all over it before I exhaled into it, "A marriage license."

He swiveled me into the seat, fastened the belt and shut the door. He gave me a wink.

We got the license and drove to his place. I hadn't been there for a over a week. We'd slept at the Sommers' house where I worked all day staging before he put it up for sale.

"Let's make some dinner," he said, leading me in the front door and through to the kitchen. We put a chicken in to roast with vegetables around it. I made an apple salad and we took glasses of wine to the back porch while the chicken roasted.

"What is that?" I pointed to the huge roof I'd noticed the other day. It rose above the grouping of conifers at the side of the lawn. A roof with a long peak overhang was constructed of metal squares a yard in size. The squares appeared to be of glass in the dark frames. A structure built out of windows didn't seem the sort of building a rancher would find practical at all. What on earth could Bull be planning to do with it?

"That's your greenhouse."

Chapter Twenty-three

We have been married for five years. We have four daughters. All have curly, black hair, brilliant blue eyes, and tiny button noses. Bull is not a father, he is a fanatic. He is the opposite of what I feared he might be—an indifferent father. He dotes on his girls. He insists on having a baby every year. I can't say no, I'm as daffy as he is about them.

When Lily, our eldest, was born he became a monster. At nighttime feeding, he was up even though I was breastfeeding. The first sound from her and he was out of bed, on his feet, telling me, "Heat the milk. I'll go get her."

He'd come back carrying her, she'd be changed and he would be crooning to her. He sat on the side of the bed while I held her in the rocking chair nursing her. When she was finished, Bull would take her from me.

"You get some sleep. I'll burp her." He would replace me in the rocking chair patting her back softly as she squirmed around while he rocked her to sleep.

Bull hired a cleaning service. My job was to grow flowers and little girls, he told me. We prepared the meals together. Lily was three months old when he began taking her with him whether he was going to the grocery, the hardware store, the auto parts store or after the mail.

When she was six months old, I was pregnant with her sister, Rose. Bull would take her to the garage with him so I could take the nap he insisted I have every afternoon. I napped more than Lily, thanks to him. Lily's naps were done on his chest. He would stretch out in the hammock I'd hung on the front porch, a canvas hammock, not string that could tangle with tiny arms and legs. We kept an afghan there for cool days. Dog always laid beneath them.

If I would waken before they did, I'd creep out to sit in the rocker and watch them. Bull's scruffy boots still made me scrunch my face in distaste after all these years. I thought about buying replacements but knew it would do no good.

Lily lay with her head beneath his chin. Bull had both hands resting on her back. The slightest move on her part made his eyes pop open. They were cute.

After Rose was six months old, the naps moved to our bedroom. Lily slept beside him, cradled in his arm and Rose on his chest. Lily was adventuresome. She was also quiet and observant like her father. Rose was boisterous, she laughed easily and often. She yelled for her Da when Bull got out of her sight. Lily would never yell. Lily would quietly search the house until she found him though, as a rule, she always knew exactly where her father was because she was with him.

Lily went to the garage with him. Rose did not. He called Lily his "little grease monkey". He read to Rose and rocked her to sleep every night to compensate for Lily's garage time. Both went to town with him. Lily rode his shoulders and Rose his arm. They were adorable.

Camellia came next. Her name was quickly shortened to Cammy. She was demonic. Cammy strained Bull's patience. Just when he was most stressed by something she'd done or wouldn't do, she'd blink her eyes at him and smile. He'd squat, open his arms and tell her, "Come to, Da." She'd giggle and run pell-mell to crash into him. When there was a spill, a mess, something out of place or missing, he would yell, "Cammy!"

She would giggle and run when she heard that yell, usually away from him. If he chased after her, she kicked her speed up a notch and laughed like the little demon she is. Cammy went to the garage once but never again.

When Bull came in the door, Cammy would run to meet him, wrap her arms around his leg, refuse to be picked up or to let go and her father limped through the house with a twenty-two pound weight on his scruffy boot.

He loved her more for the challenge she was to him. She was a different person with me. All of her questionable behavior was unleashed on her father. I like that about her.

Poppy is nine-months old. I'm pregnant.

"This is the last one, Bull. My body needs a break. You and your little harem are complete unless this is another little girl. Maybe we'll have a son this time." We were at breakfast, all of us were around the table. Poppy was in her high chair. Lily, Rose and Cammy perched on booster seats.

"Are we getting a baby?" Lily was first to ask.

"We are," said Bull, smiling at her. "We'll call her Violet."

"You don't know that the baby will be a girl, the baby may be a boy baby," I looked at their little faces as I explained to them.

"Boy." Cammy declared banging her spoon down.

"Bebe," said Poppy. She knows that word. Her father calls her baby. She is angelic.

"I had a call from the Grahams yesterday, they'd like me to come by and check the planters. I told them I'd come today if you were free to be with the children. Will today work or should I reschedule?"

The Grahams had bought the Sommers' house on sight for twice what Bull figured it would bring. He'd priced it high to give room to negotiate. They didn't blink. They wrote him a check. They hired me to come several times a year to check all the plants.

"Today is good. This morning would be better than this afternoon unless you need more time. We'll do fun stuff, won't we ladies?" He scanned the little faces smiling at the idea of fun with daddy. He was the Pied Piper and the girls adored him.

"Eat all of your breakfast and we'll get started. We'll take care of the kitchen, Mom. Take your time."

I got up, took my plate to the sink, and stooped to kiss him on my way to the bedroom to change.

"Thanks, Big Daddy."

I put on my favorite old work shorts which still fit four and a third pregnancies later. When I walked back into the kitchen in my steel-toed work boots, the shorts and my raggedy safari shirt, Bull whistled.

"Look at Mama, ladies." His arms came around me and squeezed. "I love you," he whispered in my ear.

The words took my breath away. Tears glazed over my eyes.

"I love you more." I stooped so the girls could reach me. "Kiss me, goodbye babies. Be good for Dad." I hugged each in turn and went out to drive to town.

One of the first things Bull had insisted on was that I learn to drive. He bought a van when I passed my driver's test. Of course, it was filled with baby seats. The cargo area was already loaded with my gardening tools, the most important of which was a special meter that could measure the moisture in the soil down to a depth of three feet. I would check the planters every few feet. I had prepared a watering plan for the Grahams when they bought the place.

The bougainvilleas had grown, matured and draped six-feet over the top of the fence inside and out. The cacti had flourished and the whole landscape was beautiful. It even impressed me and I'd created it. By noon, I'd finished checking the soil and ascertained that all of the plants were in excellent shape. I told the Grahams goodbye and told them to donate my fee to the Salvation Army.

The house was full of noise, laughter and screams. I could recognize Cammy's shrill screams, Poppy's deep, guttural scream. The laughter was Rose. Lily would strictly be an observer. I followed the sound to our bedroom where Bull lay splayed on the bed and the three older girls jumped up and down around him. Poppy was lying across his head hugging it with both hands.

I stood in the doorway watching until the girls noticed me and went quiet. Bull lifted Poppy off of his face and grinned at me.

"We're having a pile up, Mama."

"Pile," said Cammy and launched herself into his mid-section.

I ran to them, "Are you all right?" I crouched over him on my knees. I didn't know if Cammy had landed in the tummy or groin.

He opened one eye. "It's probably best that you don't want more children." He popped up. "Let's go, folks. It's lunchtime. Dad made spaghetti. We waited for you," he said to me.

The girls ran for the kitchen, Bull grabbed Poppy and we followed them. After lunch, we cleared the kitchen and went outside to nap. Bull and the three older girls climbed into the hammock. I sat in the rocker with Poppy over my shoulder.

I dozed off.

An engine woke me. It was Evelyn's old car. I watched as she climbed out. There was someone with her. My face froze in shock. Her passenger was Virginia McKnight, Roy's mother.

The last time I'd seen her was at Roy's trial. She was there every day according to the media. I went only when I was scheduled to testify.

The two women approached the porch.

"Afternoon, Iris. This is my new boarder, Virginia. She says she knows you and asked me to bring her by so she could say hello." Evelyn explained their presence.

"Hello, Virginia." I finally found my tongue. Why had she come? Roy was dead. He'd died several years ago, two years I think. He hadn't lasted long in prison. I remember thinking at the time that he'd probably pitched one of this tantrums at the wrong person.

"Don't speak to me you adulterous, vile bitch. I've come to take care of you, once and for all, for my poor, dead boy. You killed my baby, I'll kill yours along with you," she said, as she reached into her bag and pulled out a handgun.

"Before I shoot you and that bastard child dead, I want you to know that I intend to shoot as many of your family as possible after I kill you." She walked closer to the steps as she spoke in a calm, deadly monotone.

A sideways glance told me that Bull was awake. I could see him in my periphery. The three girls lay sleeping on top of him, pinning him down.

"You should have been a good, faithful wife to my boy. He was too good for you and you cheated on him. Now, you'll pay. At last, you'll pay." She let her purse drop and raised the gun holding it with both hands.

"Virginia!" Evelyn's voice was strident. She got Virginia's attention and she turned to see what Evelyn wanted from her.

Evelyn fired one shot and Virginia dropped to the ground. The gun clattered when it landed on the walk. Virginia made a soft thud. Evelyn tucked her smoking gun back into the large handbag over her arm.

I hadn't breathed for ever so long but my reflexes kicked in and I drew in air. One by one, Bull set the girls, who wakened at the gunfire, onto the porch and rolled out of the hammock.

"Stay right here, Ladies," he told the girls. Poppy and I were his next stop. "Are you okay, Iris?" He kissed Poppy, who was sleeping, on her cheek. I nodded and he continued past us to the steps and down to where Virginia lay.

I saw him check her neck for a pulse.

"Why don't you hand me that bag, Evelyn, and go up and have a seat with Iris. I'll call Alvin to come." He guided her past the body with his hand and mouthed to me that Virginia was dead. He made a call on his cell.

"She thought she had me fooled," said Evelyn, as she took a seat in the chair next to my rocker. "I sensed right away that she was not right, she was evil, she had bad vibes. She called me from Houston that she needed a room for a couple of nights. She had business in town, she said. She told me she has cancer and she had to take care of this business before it took her. I recognized her right off the bat, as soon as she got off the bus." Evelyn nodded, showing she'd had Virginia's number from the git go.

"I've expected her for a long time, for years. I did what I had to do to get ready as soon as the premonition came to me." She raised her brows and peered into my face. "I'd just about given up hope and figured I'd misunderstood the signs like I did that time over you and Bull. Then, the phone rang, she booked my best room, the same one you had, and things were set in motion." She nodded her head up and down again.

"Things?" I gulped.

"I knew the time had come." Her lips were stretched tight in a grim expression. "First, I cleaned the gun. It wouldn't do to have it mis-fire when you and the babies were at stake. I bought new bullets at the hardware, well, I didn't buy them. I took them. I'll go pay Fred, now that it's over. I couldn't have him alerting Alvin and ruining everything." She raised her brows higher in a "men, huh" expression.

I nodded, yes. I certainly wasn't going to argue with her. A sudden thought hit me.

"Did you use the gun from the Sommers' place? The one I found in Mr. Sommers' closet?" It had gone missing. I supposed Bull had found it and disposed of it. Guess I was wrong.

"Yes, sorry about that."

"Let's take the babies inside and make some coffee, shall we? Come with Momma, girls. Auntie Evelyn has come to have coffee with us."

Bull gave me the high sign.

"Is the lady sick?" That was Lily asking.

"Yes, baby. Daddy is going to help her."

We trooped inside, made tea and had a tea party. Evelyn, the girls and I toured the greenhouse and I asked Evelyn to pick a new rose bush for her yard.

"I'll come set it out for you."

She chose a pretty, yellow Peace rose.

Bull came and let us know the coast was clear. The Medical Examiner had come and Virginia was gone. Alvin would go to Evelyn's later to interview her. Bull had turned the weapon over to him.

"Are you sure you're all right, Iris?" He rubbed his hand over my abdomen and our growing child.

"If you and the girls are fine, then so am I."

"We need to watch Evelyn better. Did you know she had that gun?"

"No. Is she going to be prosecuted?" I couldn't bear Evelyn being jailed.

"It'll be a self-defense thing. Virginia wasn't aiming at her but Evelyn prevented a least one murder, and who knows how many of us she could have killed before I could get to her, if she hadn't plugged me first."

"Don't even say that. I can't bear the thought, especially now, at this point in my life," I said.

"Do you mean because you're pregnant?" His arms crept

around me. He had that look in his eyes like I was a vein of gold and he was a miner. It's a great look.

"Oh no, I mean because you told me you love me."

Books by Mary Kerr

marykbooks@gmail.com

INHERITED SINS
STUBBORN STANDOFF
OLD DOG, OLD TRICKS

THE KATHERINE AND HANK SERIES
PROTECTIVE CUSTODY
BOOM YOU'RE NEXT
RUBY IS RED, VIOLET IS DEAD
SWEET TIMES IN SWEET SPRINGS

MISFIT
EX AS IN EXTERMINATE
WOMAN FOR HIRE
BROTHERLY LOVE
A MAN TO DIE FOR
THE SLOANE WOMEN
REFLECTED LOVE
DIVIDED SON
ARTIFICIALLY YOURS
A DEAL IS A DEAL

AN HOUR TO LOVE BY

LOVE FOUND LOVE LOST

TALL DARK AND DIRTY

SATURDAY NIGHT IS SEX NIGHT

MILLION DOLLAR MISTRESS

JOJO'S MOJO

DEPUTY DARLING

TALK TO THE SHORTS

SAVING SUSAN

THE PERFECT LOVER

PARTNERS

BULL AND ME

SEPARATED

THE MARK OF KANE

DALLAS JONES

Made in the USA
Middletown, DE
14 October 2016